How to Write a Children's Fiction Book

Karen Cioffi

Cover Design by *100Covers.com*
Interior Design by *Formattedbooks.com*

ISBN: 978-0-9992949-1-8
LCCN: 2020903733

Contents

Section
One

Section One Content:

INTRODUCTION TO WRITING Children's Fiction
Choosing Your Target Audience
Writing Children's Books: Genre Differences
Writing Children's Books: Genres Within Genres
Finding Children's Story Ideas
Writing for Young Children: Ten Basic Rules
Critiques are Essential
Writing Conferences, Workshops, Books, Magazines, and Articles
Your Assignment

Introduction to Writing Children's Fiction

CHILDREN'S BOOKS USUALLY fall into one of three basic categories: picture books, middle grade, and young adult. To become published in any of these genres, you need to take the necessary steps to achieve success whether aiming at traditional publishing or self-publishing.

To jump into the 'writing children's fiction' arena, there are four steps needed - the first step is writing.

Actually writing, and all that it entails, is the basis of becoming a published author or writer, whether writing books, articles, becoming a ghostwriter, or copywriter. Within this first writing step, there are four subcategories.

Writing for Children: Four Traditional and 'Self' Publishing Steps – An Overview

1. Writing and Reading

The first step for a successful writing career is to write. But, simply writing isn't enough; the new writer will need to learn the craft of writing, along with the particular tricks of writing for children. Writing for children is more complicated than other forms of writing. The reason is because you're dealing with children.

Rules, such as age-appropriate words, age-appropriate topics, age-appropriate comprehension, storylines, and formatting are all features that need to be tackled when writing for children. But, the very beginning is to learn the basics of writing.

In order to learn the craft of writing, you'll need to read books and magazines relevant to learning to write. One book simply won't cut it; the topic of writing is too broad. You'll want the perspective and insight from a number of experienced authors. There are a number of resources in this book to help you in this area, and you can always ask writers in your writing groups what books they recommend.

Within this first step, aside from reading books and magazines on the craft of writing, you will need to read, read, and read in the genre you want to write. Pay special attention to recently published books and their publishers. What works in these books? What type of style is the author using? What topics/storylines are publisher's publishing?

Dissect these books, and you might even write or type them word-for-word to get a feel for writing that works. This is a trick that writers new to copywriting use – you can trick your brain into knowing the right way to write for a particular genre or field. Well, not so much trick your brain as teach it by copying effective writing. *Just remember, this is for the learning process only – you cannot use someone else's work, that's plagiarism.*

2. Writing for Children: Critiques

The next step, number two, is to become part of a critique group and have your work critiqued.

Critiquing is a two-way street: you will critique the work of other members of the critique group and they will critique yours. But, there are advantages to critiquing other writers' works – you begin to see errors quickly and notice what's being done right. This all helps you hone your craft.

Because critique groups are so important, I've included an article, "Critiques are Essential," at the end of this section.

3. Writing for Children: Revisions and Edits

Step three on the writing rung is to revise your manuscript based on your own input and that of your critique group. This process should go on until the manuscript is as good as you can get it. It's recommended to put the story away for a couple of weeks, even a couple of months, and then revisit it. You'll see a number of areas that may need tweaking and revising that you hadn't noticed before.

Then it's on to self-editing and proofreading.

4. Writing for Children: Take it to a Professional

It would also be advisable to budget for a professional editing of your manuscript before you begin submissions. No matter how careful you and your critique partners are, a working editor will pick up things you missed. If your budget just doesn't have enough for a professional edit, read everything you can on self-editing. The article links in a later section have some helpful tips. Then, apply what you've learned to your manuscript.

Once you have a polished manuscript, the next three steps in a writing career are: submissions, a contract and sales, and a writing career.

It's important to mention again that the above four steps should be taken whether you are going the traditional publishing route or you're going to self-publish.

Just because you may be by-passing the publisher's gatekeepers, who protect the integrity and quality of the work they accept, your manuscript should be the best possible, a quality product. Self-publishing is not an excuse to cut corners, rush a book, or create a substandard product. Remember that your book is a reflection of you and your writing ability.

Choosing Your Target Audience

WHEN YOU THINK of writing for children, what comes to mind?

Do you picture writing a bedtime story? Or, maybe a funny picture book? Or, maybe you think of the middle grade or young adult crowd.

What children are you envisioning reading your stories? Or are your books being read to young children, maybe babies?

Do you want to enlighten a child? Do you want to scare a child? Do you want to provide a child with a life lesson? Do you want to make a child laugh? Do you want to bring the child through a suspenseful mystery? Or do you want to take the child on a fantastic journey, broadening his imagination?

You need to think about these things when planning to write a book.

Often teachers, or parents, or grandparents, who are around children a lot, develop the desire to write for children. They might see how a child lights up when reading an engaging book. Or, they may want to spark the child's imagination and bring him or her on an amazing journey.

So, again, there's a lot to think about. Choose which age group you'd like to write for.

Being a writer, like being any kind of artist who creates something from nothing, is an amazing ability. It's almost like magic. And, you are in control. You decide what to create. *The cap on your imagination is your only limit.*

Now, we'll go over the different genres available to the children's fiction writer.

Writing Children's Books: Basic Genre Differences

THERE ARE A number of genres within the children's book arena. The target audience ranges from babies right on through to young adults. This provides a unique situation for writers to pick and choose a genre that feels comfortable to write in, while still remaining within the children's book market.

Each genre is geared toward a specific age group and has its own set of rules.

Children's Books: An overview of the different genres and a description of each:

<u>Bedtime stories</u>

These stories are simple and soothing. They are written to help lull little ones off to sleep and are in the form of picture books. The age group can be from newborn to five or six years of age.

Examples of bedtime stories include:

Day's End Lullaby by Karen Cioffi.
Good Night Moon by Margaret Wise Brown – a classic

I want to also mention a couple of Amazon's ebook listings for "bedtime picture books:"

The Magical Dragon's Three Gifts by Rachel Yu [Kindle Edition]

A Wolf Pup's Tale by Rachel Yu [Kindle Edition]

Board Books

Board books are simple picture books geared toward babies and toddlers. They are designed to hold up to a toddler's handling (including prying fingers and mouth). Board books can be black and white or very colorful. These books usually teach simple concepts, such as numbers from one to ten, days of the week, colors, and simple words.

Examples of board books are:

The Very Hungry Caterpillar by Eric Carle (a classic baby board book)

Good Night Moon by Margaret Wise Brown (another classic)

Grover's Guessing Game About Animals (a Sesame Street book)

Picture books for the 2-5 age group

These books are meant to be read aloud to the child. Rather than simply concept themes, simple story lines can be written with short sentences and words. These books are for children in the 'pre-reading' stage and the word count can range from 100 - 500 words.

Examples of this genre are:

The Runaway Bunny by Margaret Wise Brown

Where the Wild Things Are by Maurice Sendak

Fancy Nancy by Jane O'Connor (can also be in the 4-8 year old genre)

Stephanie's Ponytail by Robert Munsch (can also be in the 4-8 year old genre)

Caps for Sale by Esphyr Slobodkina (fits in the next genre also)

<u>Picture books for the 4-8 age group</u>

This genre makes up most of the picture book market. These books are also meant to be read aloud to children, but for the older child it can be read individually, as an easy or early reader. The pictures will give a visual element for children learning to read, helping with the comprehension of the text. The wording and themes can be a bit more interesting, but still rather simple.

For the writer, in this genre you will need to introduce 'showing' to create an engaging reading experience for the child. The average picture book is 32 pages and under 1000 words.

Examples of books for this age group include:

Walter the Farting Dog by William Kotzwinkle
Owen by Kevin Henkes.(can also be in the 2-5 year old genre)
Sh, Sh, Sh, Let the Baby Sleep by Kathy Stemke
Harold's Fairy Tale by Crockett Johnson
The Pea in the Peanut Butter by Allyn M. Stotz (self-published)

The last book mentioned can also fit into the 2-5-year-old group. We'll be using *The Pea in the Peanut Butter* in the workshop as a great example of an exceptionally good beginning.

Many picture books (PBs) can fit into either PB genre.

<u>Chapter books for the 6-9 or 7–10 age group</u>

Children in this group are learning to read. The vocabulary and storyline is expanding, but clarity is still a must. These books may be labeled as 'early readers' or 'easy readers' by educational publishers and are designed to be read by the child. The word count is usually between 5,000 and 12,000.

Examples of chapter books are:

Clarice Bean, that's me by Lauren Child
Because of Winn-Dixie by Kate DiCamillo.
The Boxcar Children by Gertrude Chandler Warne
The Stink Series by Megan McDonald

In regard to *Because of Winn-Dixie*, the protagonist is ten years old. **Since children tend to read-up (the protagonist will be 2 – 3 years older than the reader)**, the target audience is around 7 – 8 years old, placing it within this genre and possibly the younger end of middle grade.

Middle grade books

The middle grader is between 8 and 12 years old. The middle-grader will go for stories that he can associate with and characters he can form a bond with. The word count is usually a minimum of 20,000 to 25,000, depending on the publisher.

As the child is able to comprehend more and is maturing, so should the stories. Stories and conflict can be more involved and you can now introduce more than one protagonist or point of view. This age group can also be introduced to science fiction, fantasy, and mysteries.

Examples of middle grade books include:

Walking Through Walls by Karen Cioffi
The Lucky Baseball: My Story in a Japanese-American Internment Camp
by Suzanne Lieurance (this is considered historical fiction)
A Single Shard by Linda Sue Park
The early *Harry Potter* books by J. K. Rowling are also middle-graders.

Young adult books

This genre encompasses the twelve to sixteen and up age group. YAs can be edgy; plots and characters can be complex and serious issues addressed.

Examples of young adult books include:

An Audience for Einstein by Mark Wakely
The Rock of Realm by Lea Schizas
The Kane Chronicles by Rick Riordan
The *Twilight* series by Stephenie Meyer
The latter books in the *Harry Potter* series

A useful way to get a better idea of what the different genres consist of is to visit your local library and talk to the children's section librarian. She'll be able to show you books in each genre and give you tidbits of information on which are the most popular, which are classic, and much more.

A note: Many books can fall under two different genres. For example, *Fancy Nancy* is categorized for ages 4 and up, so can fit into two genres. Other examples are *Winn-Dixie* and *The Pea in the Peanut Butter*, as well as *Walking Through Walls* (it's also consider a YA). And, depending on the publisher, the word counts for genres can vary somewhat.

A final note: Ebooks and self-publishing are changing the face of children's writing. Authors now have the means to publish without the long, drawn-out process of traditional publishing. But, as mentioned in the Introduction to this course, this is not a 'pass go' card that provides leeway for unprofessional and unpolished books. No matter what publishing path you choose, take the time to do it right.

For a bit more on book genres check out these two articles:

Identifying Genre
  http://kidlit.com/2012/03/05/identifying-genre/

The Difference Between School Readers and Picture Books
  http://robynopie.blogspot.com/2009/08/claire-saxbys-sheep-goat-and-creaking.html

If you have the paperback version of this book, you can find clickable links for the LINKS throughout this book at:

http://karencioffiwritingforchildren.com/writing-fiction-for-children-articles/
(Please do not share this link – it's for those who purchase the book only.)

Writing Children's Fiction Books: Genres Within Genres

FROM THE PREVIOUS pages, you can see that genres consist of books for different age groups. But there are also different subject matter within those genres.

Here is a list of some of the subject matter genres for children's writing. Some may be used for all of the age groups, while others will be specific to picture book, chapter, middle grade, and/or young adult.

Subject matter genres include:

Adventure
Comic
Crime
Docufiction
Epistolary
Faction
Fantasy
Historical Fiction
Horror
Mystery
Philosophical

Poetry
Romance
Saga
Satire
Science Fiction
Superhero
Tragedy
Thriller/Suspense
Urban
Westerns

To get a feel for the different genres, go to your library and ask the librarian for books on the various subject matters. Take the time to check a number of them out - you never know, you may develop a liking for one or two you're unfamiliar with.

Finding Children's Story Ideas

SITTING AT THE computer with a blank word document in front of you may be intimidating for a writer.

Hmmm. What should the story be about? You think and think. You gaze out the window. You draw a blank.

Alexander Steele wrote a short article in the October 2010 issue of *The Writer*, "Where can you find the seeds of a good story?" It was interesting to read that Herman Melville, author of *Moby-Dick*, had his own whaling adventures which he used to create a wonderful, everlasting story. Steele advices, "Probably the most fertile place to look for ideas is right inside the backyard of your own life."

You might be thinking you don't have close contact with children, so you don't have any experiences to draw on. Or, you may be so busy living your life and raising your children that you don't have time to stop and notice all the amazing story opportunities that are right in your own backyard. Well, even if these scenarios fit, you can take steps to rectify the situation.

Karen Cioffi

Some want-to-be authors get up an hour early, before the family morning be-gins, to get some writing in (and this include coming up with ideas). Some stay up an hour later. Where there's a will, there's a way.

Finding Story Ideas if You *Don't* Have Close Contact with Children

1. Turn on the TV. Yes, this is an excellent source for story ideas, as well as watching children's behavior. While it may be in the confines of a scripted show, the writers of these shows try to keep it as 'real' as possible. Take note of the situations, the attitudes of the actors, the scenes, and everything else. Even children's cartoons have engaging storylines. It may be just the spark you need.

2. Go to a playground with notebook in hand. Watch the children play and listen to them talk. If you're a professional writer (ghostwriter), or you're already published, consider asking your local age appropriate school if you could sit in the lunchroom during lunch periods. A useful way to get a positive answer would be to first ask if you could give an author or writing presentation to the students. The principal would need to be sure you are a legitimate writer. Please note though, there may be legal and safety aspects a school would need to consider.

Note: If you do go to a playground or other area where there are children, be sure to inform parents/guardians of what you're doing. It'd be a good idea to bring a copy of one of your published stories, articles, or books with you, so they feel comfortable that you are indeed a writer. It's a crazy world, always take precautions, and keep the safety of our children at the forefront.

3. Read newly published children's books, and reread ones you enjoyed as a child, then reinvent a story. This is a tip I took advantage of with my own children's fantasy book, *Walking Through Walls*. I read an ancient Chinese tale and reinvented it for a children's book. During a teleclass, I was recently reminded of this story idea source by multi-published children's writer Margot Finke.

Finke advised to study books you like; pay attention to why they work, then "craft an entirely new story." She explained that, "quirky and fresh" wins publishing contracts today.

Finding Story Ideas if You *Do* Have Close Contact with Children

1. Study the children you do have contact with, whether your own children, your grandchildren, or other relatives. Children are an amazing source of inspiration and ideas. They have an innate ability to make you feel. Just looking at a picture of children may make you smile; hearing a baby laugh can actually make you laugh.

Watch the children, notice their mannerisms, body language, movements, attitudes and emotions, speech, and their interactions with other children and adults. You'll not only get story ideas, you'll also get dialogue and 'showing' descriptions.

2. If you have regular contact with children, you really shouldn't need any other steps, but if the age of your new story differs from the ages of the children you see, use the steps noted above for writers who don't have contact with children.

Writing for Young Children: Ten Basic Rules

I WRITE FOR children and I also write marketing and health articles. Writing in multiple genres, I can tell you that writing for children can be much more challenging. When writing for children, there are guidelines to keep in mind to help your story avoid the editor's trash pile. Here is a list of ten rules to refer to when writing for young children:

1. This is probably the most important item: be sure that your story does not suggest dangerous or inappropriate behavior.

Example: The protagonist (main character) sneaks out of the house while his parents are still sleeping.

This is a no-no!

2. Make sure your story has age appropriate words, dialogue and action.

Example: You put the word 'fragile' in your manuscript, is it age appropriate for a third grader?

3. The protagonist should have an age appropriate problem or dilemma to solve at the beginning of the story, in the first paragraph if possible. Let the action/conflict rise. Then have the protagonist, through thought process and problem-solving skills, solve it on his/her own. If an adult is involved, keep the input and help at a bare minimum.

Kid's love action and problem solving!

4. The story should have a single point of view (POV). To write with a single point of view means that if your protagonist can't see, hear, touch, taste, or feel it, it doesn't exist.

Example: "Mary crossed her eyes behind Joe's back." If Joe is the protagonist this can't happen because Joe wouldn't be able to see it.

5. Sentence structure: Keep sentences short and as with all writing, keep adjectives and adverbs to a minimum. And, watch your punctuation and grammar.

6. Write your story by showing through action and dialogue rather than telling.

If you can't seem to get the right words to show a scene, try using dialogue instead; it's an easy alternative. Just don't overdo it.

7. You also need to keep your writing tight. This means don't say something with ten words if you can say it with five. Get rid of unnecessary words.

Example: Watch for the overuse of the words such 'was.'

8. Watch the timeframe for the story. Try to keep it within several hours or one day.

9. Your protagonist needs to grow. Along with the protagonist's solution to the conflict, she/he needs grow in some way as a result.

10. Use a thesaurus and book of similes. Finding just the right word or simile can make the difference between a good story and a great story.

Using these techniques will help you create effective children's stories. Another important tool to use in your writing tool belt is joining a children's writing critique group, as mentioned earlier.

No matter how long you've been writing, you can always use another set of eyes.

It you're a beginning writer and unpublished, you should join a group that has published and unpublished members. Having published and experienced writers in the group will help you hone your craft.

Critiques Are Essential

As an editor, former moderator of a children's writing critique group, and a reviewer for multiple genres, I read a number of manuscripts and books. Reading both well written books and books that lack polish, it's easy to tell which authors haven't bothered to have their work critiqued or edited.

Seeing the unnecessary and unprofessional mistakes of writers publishing unpolished work, I always include the importance of belonging to a critique group in articles or ebooks I write about writing. Even experienced authors depend on the unique perspective and extra eyes that each critique member provides.

The critique group can catch a number of potential problems in your manuscript, such as:

1. Grammatical errors
2. Holes in your story
3. Unclear sentences, paragraphs, or dialogue
4. The forward movement of the story
5. Overuse of a particular word, or too many adjectives and adverbs
6. Unnecessary words to eliminate for a tight story

The list goes on and on. And, there are even more potential problems to be watched for when writing for children. It's almost impossible for even an experienced writer to catch all of his or her own errors.

Your critique partners will also provide suggestions and guidance. Note here, it is up to you whether to heed those suggestion and comments, but if all the members of your group suggest you rewrite a particular sentence for clarity, hopefully a light will go off (in your head) and you'll pay attention.

Along with having those extras sets of eyes to help you along, you will begin to see your own writing improve. You will also be able to find your own errors and those of others much quicker. This will help you become a better and more confident writer.

Now, while the critique group does not take the place of an editor, they do help you get to the point where you think you're ready for submission. At this point, it is always advisable to seek a professional editor, if at all possible, to catch what you and your critique group missed. There will definitely be something in your manuscript that wasn't picked up on.

When joining a critique group, be sure the group has both new and experienced writers. The experienced writers will help you hone your craft through their critiques of your work. I highly recommend you join a critique group.

Writing Conferences, Workshops, Magazines, Books, and Articles

As YOU BEGIN your writing journey, it's important to understand that there is much involved in writing. And, honing your writing craft will be an ongoing project.

This book will give you what's needed to write your children's story and submit it, but as with any craft, there's always more to learn. So, I'm including a number of writing conferences, workshops, books, and magazines you can look into.

WRITING CONFERENCES:

The Guide to Writers Conferences & Workshops
http://writing.shawguides.com/

Top 10 Writing Conferences in North America
https://www.writermag.com/2017/01/17/top-10-writing-conferences-north-america/
(Past 2017, look for current conferences on the site)

Writing Conferences and Events
https://www.newpages.com/writers-resources/writing-conferences-events

The Write Life
https://thewritelife.com/writers-conferences/

WRITING WORKSHOPS, VIDEOS, and CLASSES:

Savvy Authors
http://www.savvyauthors.com/vb/blog.php

WOW! Women on Writing
http://wow-womenonwriting.com/WOWclasses.html

WRITING GROUPS

Society of Children's Book Writers and Illustrators
https://www.scbwi.org/

JacketFlap
http://www.jacketflap.com

Connects you to the work of more than 200,000 authors, illustrators, publishers and other creators of books for Children and Young Adults

AuthorsDen
http://authorsden.com

Where authors and reader come together - more than a million readers every month

You can also do an online search for online writing groups and/or children's online writing groups through Yahoo, or other email provider.

MAGAZINES

The Writer
Writer's Digest
Writer's Chronicle

Poets and Writers

BOOKS ON WRITING REFERENCED IN THIS COURSE

HOOKED
Author: Les Edgerton, from Writer's Digest Books
About novel writing, beginnings in particular

Second Sight: An Editor's Talks on Writing, Revising, and Publishing Books for Children and Young Adults
Author: Cheryl B. Klein

Story Engineering
Author: Larry Brooks
Mastering the six core competencies of successful writing

Crafting Scenes
Author: Raymond Obstfeld

ARTICLES TO GET YOU STARTED:

Benefits of Outlining
http://www.helpingwritersbecomeauthors.com/benefits-of-outlining/

The Basics of Plot: A Classical Approach
http://educationwantstobefree.blogspot.com/2011/09/basics-of-plot-classical-approach.html

This is just the tip of the writing resource iceberg. As you join writing groups ask the experienced authors and writers for 'writing resources' they recommend.

There will be more writing resources in the Bonus Section at the end of this course.

NOTE: For those who purchased the paperback, there are clickable links to all the articles in this book at:

http://karencioffiwritingforchildren.com/writing-fiction-for-children-articles/

This is a private URL – please do not share it.

Your Assignment for Section One

— — — — — — — — — — — — — — —

Go to the library and browse through the different children's genres. Ask the librarian which are the most popular genres and within each genre which are the most popular books.

Decide what genre you want to write in. Remember, this is not set in stone . . . this is just the beginning.

Read, read, read, read, read, read, read . . .

Books that will be used as examples throughout the sections:

Walking Through Walls by Karen Cioffi, a middle grade fantasy adventure (used extensively for analysis – awarded the Children's Literary Classics Silver Award 2012 and won first place in the Predators and Editors Reading Poll, Children's Novel category 2012)

Stephanie's Ponytail by Robert Munscha picture book, (used rather extensively for analysis)

The Pea in the Peanut Butter by Allyn M. Stotz, a picture book

A Single Shard by Linda Sue Park, a middle grade book (Newbery Medal)

The Lucky Baseball by Suzanne Lieurance, a middle grade historical fiction

Because of Winn-Dixie by Kate DiCamillo, a chapter book (Newberry Honor)

Caps for Sale by Esphyr Slobodkina, a picture book

While you don't have to buy any of these books, it'd be advisable to borrow them from the library so you can follow along with the analysis, especially for the two used extensively.

Section
Two

Grabbing Your Reader's Attention

TODAY, THE READER *needs to be 'hooked' and entertained right away, especially the young reader. The beginning of the book is the 'do or die' part. This section will teach you how to begin your story and 'grab' your audience.*

Section Two Content:

The Story Beginning Basics
Story Beginning Examples
Creating a Story: Two Different Formulas
Rewriting a Folktale
Your Assignment

There is a great deal that goes into writing for children, into learning to write in general, and it would be impossible for this course to cover it all. So, in addition to each Section's topic, I've included related information that will add to your understanding of writing for children.

The Story Beginning Basics

THERE'S NO WAY of getting around this, you need to have a 'grabbing' beginning to your story; this is also called a 'narrative hook.' And, that hook should start in your very first sentence. This is what will 'grab' and 'hook' the reader in.

Having a beginning that makes the reader want to keep reading is essential for two reasons:

1. It will encourage the child to want to read your book. Today's lightning fast society warrants an immediate 'hook.' Kids are used to having immediate gratification, whether through video, CDs, or TV.

According to an article at USAToday.com, "So much media, so little attention span," both school psychologists and teachers find that more and more children can't seem to sit still. David Walsh, an educational psychologist, said, "It's become harder over the last 10 years to keep kids' attention. The expectation is to be constantly entertained and, if they're not entertained, they quickly lose interest."

The article goes on to say that "the problem intensifies after third grade."

You can see that 'grabbing' the reader at the get-go is essential.

2. If you're going the traditional route, it will usually be the determining factor as to whether or not the gatekeeper (the editor or agent who receives your manuscript) will decide to invest in it.

And, the gatekeeper most often will only skim read your first page, possibly only read your first paragraph, so you MUST make it count.

Once you hook the reader in, the rest of your story will need to sustain her interest.

So, how exactly do you begin your story and captivate your reader?

One good way to get an idea of how to structure a "grabbing' beginning is to analyze what works. As mentioned in the Introduction, read what's being published. This will certainly give you a guideline as to what agents and publishers are looking for in today's books. There are also examples in the following pages.

Along with this, you will need to know that there are three basic elements to a children's story: **character, setting, and plot.** They work together to weave an engaging story, right through to the end.

There are also general guidelines to the children's book itself – knowing these guidelines will help you write the beginning. The guidelines are:

The Beginning: The set-up and introduction of the protagonist

In the beginning you'll introduce your protagonist, your main character (MC), and you will need to find a way to make the reader care about him or her. You might also bring in other characters, including the antagonist (the MC's trouble–maker).

The beginning of your book is where you will also set up the dilemma or problem the MC faces. You might use an inciting incident here – something that triggers the initial problem. The beginning is the lead-in to your story. It's what will make the reader want to find out what happens, causing him to read on.

The Problem: Obstacles or complications

This element of the story establishes the actual problem or complication the MC faces. In this section, you can add up to three stepping stones or obstacles for the MC to overcome, depending on the genre you're writing in. When one is overcome, the next one pops up.

Protagonist's Choices or Paths

Here the MC will make choices that will lead to fulfilling his wants or needs, or overcome his problem and related obstacles. Usually the choices or decisions made will cause him to grow in some way; maybe he'll become wiser, smarter, stronger . . . In fact, in every good children's book, the MC changes in a positive way as a result of overcoming the obstacles and problem.

Tie It All Together – Your Ending

Your ending will tie your story together. Any innuendos you planted in the story need to be brought into the open and resolved – there can be NO loose ends. The ending should provide a satisfying conclusion for the reader.

Now that you understand the basis of a children's story, let's get into creating an 'out of the ballpark' beginning.

IN THE BEGINNING

According to Les Edgerton, in his book Hooked, the beginning of your story has a huge responsibility and has <u>four specific goals and fundamental elements all working together to hook your reader:</u>

1. It must effectively introduce the "story-worthy problem" through an inciting incident.
2. The 'problem' must hook the readers.
3. It "establishes the rules of the story."
4. It hints at the story's ending.

There's also number 5: it introduces your protagonist.

Other elements of your beginning not mentioned yet are: backstory, setting, and language.

Let's go over each of these five elements, noting that elements 2 and 4 are included in the set-up:

Character Introduction

Introducing your protagonist in the very first paragraph is essential for children's stories, especially for young children. It's the relationship the reader develops with the character that will make your books a success.

You can also introduce the antagonist in the beginning – he's the problem-maker for the protagonist.

The Initial Obstacle/Problem or Inciting Incident

The inciting incident may be an occurrence or other event that establishes the protagonist's initial problem. This introduces the first hint of the trouble ahead.

For the younger genres the inciting incident or the problem itself needs to be established very early on. For the older-end of middle grade and young adult, the beginning may simply set up a scene and introduce the protagonist and possibly the secondary character/s.

The Set-up

In the very beginning of your story you will set up the plot. This will establish what will happen on the next page or in the next chapter of the book. This is needed so that the reader doesn't have to play catch-up or stop to backtrack as he moves forward in your story. The reader needs to be aware of what's going on every step of the way.

You don't want the reader to pause, wondering how he got there. If you don't forewarn or create a preview of what's to come, the reader will pause.

This pause may be small and cause a simple hiccup, or it can be significant and cause a major cough. If it's the latter, you can lose your reader.

One BIG tip for any of your writing: Don't make the reader pause.

In *Walking Through Walls*, the first page sets up the plot: Wang doesn't want to slave in the wheat fields like his father. He has higher goals and the Eternals are involved.

The set-up will also establish the language, style, setting, and possibly backstory.

The overall rule of the set-up "is to only give what's absolutely necessary for the reader to understand the scene that will follow and no more" (*Hooked*, 27).

Establishing the Rules of the Story

The rules of the story are set by you, the author. You decide on what to write. It may be a comedy, a drama, a science fiction, or other genre, that will create the tone and voice of the story. The 'rule' here is not to break your own rule.

This means if you're writing a period piece, like my middle grade story *Walking Through Walls*, which is set in 16th century China, you must remain in the period. Let's use an example from the book (this is the first paragraph):

Wang bound the last bunch of wheat stalks as the sun beat down on the field. Sweat poured from the back of his neck drenching the cotton shirt he wore. *I hate doing this work.* He hurled the bundles on a cart. "Father, the bales are stacked. I am going home; it is too hot."

This is the first paragraph of *Walking Through Walls* and in a few sentences, it establishes the story's rules:

It is a period piece: The name used, speech, and the context of the paragraph reflect the tone and voice of the story.

Notice there are no contractions: "I am" is used in place of "I'm;" "it is" is used in place of "it's."

If I had switched mid-story to contemporary speech and names, it would throw the readers off. I'd be breaking my own rules.

In addition to this, there are three fundamental factors to all good children's fiction: (1) there must be a clear-cut point of view, (2) there must be a lot of conflict, and (3) to bring the story to life, all the sensory details need to be used. We'll discuss this more in a later section.

There you have the basic structure of the beginning of a story.

One final note here: Children's books up to, and most often through simpler middle-grade (for the eight and nine-year-old, and the reluctant reader), are generally told from a single point of view (POV). Children don't understand as adults do, so concepts and points of view need to be simplified. There's more on POV below.

We'll use examples of traditionally published and self-published books to get an idea of great beginnings

Story Beginning Examples

FIRST UP is a picture book mentioned in Section One, *The Pea in the Peanut Butter* by Allyn M. Stotz. This can fall into the 2 – 5 age group and the 4 – 8 age group.

The book is self-published and has a couple of flaws, but the beginning has an 'out of the ballpark' hook that keeps kids coming back to read it over and over. I know because my grandsons absolutely love it.

Here is the very first sentence of the book:

I love the super, duper, gummy, yummy, sticky licken', and belly rubbin' taste of peanut butter.

Say it out loud a couple of times and you'll get the sense of what kids love about this one sentence. As you read it you can hear the MC's excitement over peanut butter and the words are just *fun*. In one sentence the author grabs the child.

The next two sentences are just as good and bring the reader further in:

If Mommy would let me, I'd spread it on hot dogs, fish sticks, chips, and pancakes. I'd eat it on bananas, grapes, apples, and frosted flakes.

You can actually hear the MC's passion, her love of peanut butter. The author does an excellent job of bringing that passion right off the page. You're feeling the MC's emotions directly. That's good writing.

In the last two sentences of the first page Stotz introduces the worthy-problem:

"Can I have more peanut butter, Mommy?"
Mommy shook her head. "No more peanut butter until you learn to like other foods."

There you have it, a first page that pretty much does it all: the protagonist is introduced, it's a slam-dunk beginning, and it introduces the inciting incident, the hint of the conflict.

The author definitely knows her audience, her target market. Kids in this intended age group love the silly words, the tongue-twisters, the excitement, the idea of what the MC is saying. And, the book has amazing illustrations that complement and add to the text, as they should.

There are a couple of other pointers about this first page, including point of view and quotation punctuation for paragraphs, that I'd like to discuss.

I don't mean to get sidetracked here, but this is important information.

1. Point of View (POV)

Point of view is the perspective of the story teller and there are no rules telling authors what tense or perspective to use for children's stories.

The types of POV are:

Objective Point of View – The author/narrator tells the story only through its action and dialogue.

First Person Point of View - The MC is narrator and telling his own story. This POV works very well with children's stories. It's as if the MC is talking directly to the reader – it's a stronger voice. **But, it's a bit tricky to write, compared to third person.** In first person the words "I" and "my" are used in conveying the story. "I fell over my bike."

Third Person POV – The narrator tells the story, but is not one of the characters. The reader learns about the characters and their feelings through the narrator. The words "he" and "she" and "they" are used to convey the story. "He fell over his bike."

Omniscient and Limited Omniscient POV – The narrator knows it all. He knows everything about each character. He's all knowing.

If the narrator's knowledge is limited to one character, he has limited omniscient POV.

The teachers' resource site Annenberg Learner gives an excellent explanation of POV
    (http://www.learner.org/interactives/literature/read/pov1.html):

An automobile accident occurs. Two drivers are involved. Witnesses include four sidewalk spectators, a policeman, a man with a video camera who happened to be shooting the scene, and the pilot of a helicopter that was flying overhead. Here we have nine different points of view and, most likely, nine different descriptions of the accident.

In short fiction, who tells the story and how it is told are critical issues for an author to decide. The tone and feel of the story, and even its meaning, can change radically depending on who is telling the story.

The Pea in the Peanut Butter is told in First Person.

One important factor to remember when writing in first person and third person is that the MC must witness everything that goes on in the story. If he doesn't see, hear, feel, smell, taste, or touch it, it doesn't belong in the story.

<u>To demonstrate:</u> John is the protagonist:

John walked home dragging his backpack along the ground. When he got to the corner a car whizzed by almost hitting the curb. John stumbled back and fell.

The driver smirked as he sped away.

Since this content is from John's POV, the last sentence can't be used – it's switching the POV to the driver. Unless of course, John saw what the drive did. Let's reword it:

John walked home dragging his backpack along the ground. When he got to the corner a car whizzed by almost hitting the curb. John stumbled back and fell. As the driver sped away, John saw him look back and laugh.

We have the same scenario, but now it's all within John's POV and acceptable.

2. Punctuation When Quoting Paragraphs

When quoting the first page above, I put the text in a box, so didn't need to use quotation marks, but I want to show you how it should be written without the boxes:

"I love the super, duper, gummy, yummy, sticky licken', and belly rubbin' taste of peanut butter.

"If Mommy would let me, I'd spread it on hot dogs, fish sticks, chips, and pancakes."

As you can see in the above example, when a character's dialog continues into the next paragraph, the first paragraph does NOT get a closing quotation mark. The second paragraph gets an opening quotation mark. The closing quotation mark goes at the end of the last paragraph of the dialog.

This works the same if the character's dialog continues into three or more paragraphs.

Okay, back on track.

THE NEXT EXAMPLE of a 'grabbing' beginning is the middle grade book *Because of Winn-Dixie* by Kate DiCamillo.

Below are the first two paragraphs:

My name is India Opal Buloin, and last summer my daddy, the preacher, sent me to the store for a box of macaroni-and-cheese, some white rice, and two tomatoes and I came back with a dog. This is what happened: I walked into the produce section of the Winn-Dixie grocery store to pick up two to-matoes and I almost bumped right into the store manager. He was standing there all red-faced, screaming and waving his arms around.

"Who let a dog in here?" he kept on shouting. "Who let a dirty dog in here?"

From what we learned previously, this story is told in first person POV, and right off the bat you're told the MC's name and that her father is a preacher. Also note that she's talking directly to the reader, telling the reader what's going on (the opening situation).

This is considered a situation beginning. Then she backtracks to let you know how it came about – this is a great way to create an instant connection.

Note: *Walking Through Walls* is a situation beginning also.

Back to Winn-Dixie: Look at all the information the author packed into one first sentence.

To further hook the reader, Opal tells us she was to go to the store for food, but ended up with a dog. That's a great twist and a lot of fun for the reader. It also makes the reader want to know more about Opal and her new dog.

The first paragraph also gives us insight into Opal's character. She's not a meek child--she tells it like it is.

The next page goes on tell of the dog's mischief-making in the store and that the manager was overwhelmed:

"Please," said the manager, "Somebody call the pound."
"Wait a minute!" I hollered. "That's my dog. Don't call the pound."

Now you see another facet of Opal's character, she's kind hearted, protects those in need, and has no qualms about telling a lie.

At the end of the brief first chapter, Opal tells the reader about the dog:

He smiled at me. He did that thing again, where he pulled back his lips and showed me his teeth. He smiled so big that it made him sneeze. It was like he was saying, "I know I'm a mess. Isn't it funny?"
It's hard not to immediately fall in love with a dog who has a good sense of humor.
"Come on," I told him, "Let's see what the preacher has to say about you."

Within one short chapter, you're hooked. You've found out that Opal's funny, caring, and tough. And, you want to read on. Everything is in place in this story's beginning.

Note: It's often advised to create an action first sentence. This can be done through dialogue, action, or other hooking sentence.

Here are a few first sentences; some include the first two sentences:

The Kissing Hand by Audrey Penn (New York Times #1 Bestseller)

Chester Raccoon stood at the edge of the forest and cried. "I don't want to go to school," he told his mother."

The Single Shard by Linda Sue Park (Winner of the John Newbery Medal)

"Eh, Tree-ear! Have you hungered well today?" Crane-man called out as Tree-ear drew near the bridge.

Stephanie's Ponytail by Robert Munsch

One day Stephanie went to her mom and said, "None of the kids in my class have a ponytail. I want a nice ponytail coming right out the back."

Middle School, The Worst Years of My Life by James Patterson

It feels as honest as the day is crummy that I begin this tale of total desperation and woe with me, my pukey sister, Georgia, and Leonardo the Silent sitting like rotting sardines in the back of a Hills Village Police Department cruiser.

Diary of a Wimpy Kid: Cabin Fever by Jeff Kinney
Amazingly popular book series, at least one became a movie.

November, Saturday: Most people look forward to the holidays, but the stretch between Thanksgiving and Christmas just makes me a nervous wreck. If you make a mistake in the first eleven months of the year, it's no big deal. But, if you do something wrong during the holiday season, you're going to pay for it.

(I added the third line of the quote from *Diary of a Wimpy Kid* because the paragraph is just so good. What kid wouldn't relate to this and want to continue reading?)

For more insight into what makes an exceptional first line, check out 100 Best First Lines of Novels: http://www.infoplease.com/ipea/A0934311.html

Additional Resources:

First Lines – Part 1
http://kidlit.com/2011/07/25/first-lines-part-1/
Check out all the First Line Parts from Mary Kole, a children's agent

Fix Your Beginning
http://kidlit.com/2009/12/07/fix-your-beginning/

Memorable First Lines
http://joanyedwards.wordpress.com/2012/04/18/memorable-first-lines/

Kidlit.com is a site to check on regularly.

Creating a Story: Two Different Formulas

WHILE THIS SECTION discusses the beginning of your story, I want to also mention that there are two different formulas for creating a story.

Every writer has a personal writing style—it's unique, the same is true of the writing process. If you ask ten authors their process for writing a children's story, odds are you'll get ten different answers. Writing is a very personal journey. While a writer may have a different style and use different processes, within those processes are common formulas.

I would venture to say that the most popular formula is creating an outline. But there are also writers who use the seat-of-the-pants formula. Each of these two formulas will bring you to the same end-result, they just use different means. Before discussing them though, the first thing on the agenda is the *idea*. Every journey begins with the first step; the writing journey's first step is the *story idea*.

The Idea

So, you want to write a children's story, but what will it be about? Ideas and inspiration are all around us. Children you know, children on TV or in movies, children at a playground, at the beach, anywhere you can see or hear children can be a source for an idea. Watch their actions, their interactions and reactions; if you can hear them, listen to their language. All of this will help you later on as you're actually writing your story.

It might be helpful to make a list of all the ideas you come up with and then do a process of elimination. Choose the one you feel most inspired about. Be sure to save the other ideas for possible, future stories.

Many writers keep pads or notebooks with them all the time, in case they come across something that sparks an idea and might make a good story. Rather than leaving it to memory, they quickly write it down. Or, easier yet, make note of it on your smart phone.

What might a story idea be?

Thinking of *Thelma and Louise*, maybe the author's initial idea was that two friends decide to go on a trip and something happens.

Once you have the initial idea, you expand on it with questions:

- Where are the friends going?
- What happens?
- What kind of trouble do they get into?
- Does the trouble escalate? If so, how?
- How do they get out of the trouble?
- Do they get out of the trouble?
- How does the story end?

You can always use the "what if" to expand on each of the questions.

Okay, you have your story idea. Now it's time to write a draft of your story.

NOTE: A draft is your working story. The first draft is where you write without your inner critic. Just let the story flow – don't worry about editing it at this point. Once your story is polished and edited, it's called a manuscript.

There are two methods to write drafts.

The Outline Formula

With your idea in hand, you will now let it blossom like a flower; let it open, one petal than another, each bringing more detail and beauty. First the beginning unravels flowing into middle and then into the end. These are the essential parts of every story.

Create these three sections then open each of them up—let them blossom. Pretty soon you'll have an entire outline for a story. Next, you'll use the outline to create a story.

This process offers a sense of security. It's like having a roadmap in front of you: go to Exit 5 then head north to Lincoln Street. You know where you're going - it's just matter of how quickly you can get there. Maybe you encounter a traffic jam or you get a flat tire. Whatever obstacle gets in your way, you have a definite destination.

An outline affords stepping stones, one leads into the next. This structure helps you to craft the beginning to meld into the middle, and the middle into the end. There is comfort in knowing where your next step will be. Even if you need to change pertinent aspects in the story, such as adding a character, or even the basic structure somewhat, you still have a rough roadmap to help you get to that final destination.

It's important to keep in mind that your outline can change as you go along. An author friend of mine uses sticky notes for different scenes/events/characters. If she revises something, she removes or adds a sticky note.

The Seat-of-the-Pants Formula (Organic formula)

This formula may be a little scary, staring at a screen with just an idea at the top, waiting for something to appear. But while it's a little intimidating, it offers a sense of the unknown and adventure. You stare at your idea and then suddenly you have a sentence or two that automatically takes you into another sentence or two, and then another, and yet another. Before you know it, you're typing away. To witness the creation of characters, personalities, and even worlds born from your imagination is thrilling.

I have used both formulas to write stories for children and I find using the outline formula is more comfortable. I like having a clear direction to head in and knowing where I need to turn. But interestingly, I find myself repeatedly using the seat-of-the pants method.

The writing process is a personal journey - you'll have to determine which formula works best for you.

Sitting on Your Draft

Okay, this doesn't mean literally, it means once your draft is complete it's time to pause. Take a vacation from it for few days to a couple of weeks then go back to it with fresh eyes. This will help you to find areas that need revisions.

One other bit of information I want to add to this section is about story verb tense.

You can write in present tense or past tense.

Simple present tense/Third person POV: He is <u>going</u> to the store.
Past tense/Third person POV: He <u>went</u> to the store.

Present: Wang <u>wants</u> to be rich and powerful.
Past: Wang <u>wanted</u> to be rich and powerful.

Whichever tense you use, stick with it. You must be consistent throughout the story.

For a closer look at verb tenses, check out:
http://www.edufind.com/english/grammar/summary_of_verb_tenses.php

Rewriting a Folktale: Walking Through Walls

WHEN A WRITER'S *muse* seems to be on vacation, she may be at a loss for story ideas. While there are a number of sites and tools online to help get the creative juices flowing, one tool that writers might overlook is studying folktales.

Reading folktales is a great way to spin a new yarn, especially for children's writing. I recently did a review of a children's picture book published by Sylvan Dell that was based on an American Indian folktale. This shows they are publishable.

Folktales, also known as tall tales, and folklore, are stories specific to a country or region. They are usually short stories dealing with everyday life that come from oral tradition that is passed on from generation to generation. Most often these tales involve animals, heavenly objects, and other non-human entities that possess human characteristics.

There is Mexican folklore, Irish folklore, Chinese folklore, as well as folklore from many other countries that have tales unique to their area. There is also American folklore that encompasses stories from each of the 50 states. There is a huge supply of stories to spin and weave.

In addition to reviewing a couple of published children's books that were based on folktales, I wrote a children's fantasy story based on an ancient Chinese tale.

Interestingly, prior to receiving an outline of the tale from a Chinese nonfiction writer acquaintance, I never thought of rewriting folktales. But once given the outline I loved the story and the message it presented. The outline itself was very rough and written with an adult as the main character (MC). This is often the case with ancient folktales.

After reading the story I knew the MC would need to become a child. Every children's writer is aware that children want to read about children, not adults. And the MC needs to be a couple of years older than the target audience the author is writing for.

Based on this, the MC became a 12-year-old boy. And, since the ancient Chinese flavor of the story seemed perfect, I kept it and made the story take place in the 16th century China. After these two factors were set, a title and the MC's name needed to be created.

When choosing a title for your book, it's important to keep it in line with the story and make it something that will be marketable to the age group you're targeting. I chose *Walking Through Walls*.

As far as the character's name, you will need to base it on the time period and geographic location of the story, unless the character is out of his element. Since my story takes place in China, the MC needed a Chinese name.

To keep the flavor of your story consistent, you will also need to give it a feeling of authenticity. This will involve some research:

How did the people dress during the time period of your story? What names were used? What did they eat? What type of work or schooling was available? What locations might you mention? What type of crops and vegetation would be present? What types of homes did they live in?

There are many aspects of the story that you will want to make as authentic as possible. And it does matter, even in fiction stories. It will add richness to your story.

The next time you're in the library, ask the librarian to show you a few folktales. Then imagine how you might rewrite one or more of them for today's children's book market.

Section Two Assignment

1. HOPEFULLY, YOU took out some popular children's books from the library for Section One. Carefully read the first sentences, first paragraphs, and first few pages or first chapter. Study them and try to figure out why they work and take notice of the elements of a 'grabbing' beginning in them.

If you didn't take any books out yet, go to the library and ask the librarian for popular children's books and award-winning children's books. Pay special attention to those recently published.

2. Having decided what genre you want to begin writing in, write a ONE page beginning. (*For manuscript purposes, one page consists of approximately 250 words, double spaced, and in Arial, Times New Roman, or Veranda font. The first line of each paragraph should be indented.*)

This one page will include your protagonist's name, the setting, the tone, the inciting incident, the hint of or the actual problem, and the other elements of a good beginning.

Okay, include as many elements as you can. Is that better?

It's not a test, so don't get nervous.

Just do your best and have fun with it.

3. If you haven't joined a critique group yet, do it now. Then, according to their guidelines, submit your paragraph for critique.

Section
Three

Building Characters and Dialogue

IS YOUR CHARACTER *one-dimensional, two-dimensional, or three-dimensional? Characters need to have a life-like personality in order to engage and connect with the reader. Along with this, dialogue needs to be believable. In this section, we'll examine what it means to create believable characters and dialogue. We'll also touch on other facets of your story.*

Section Three Content:

Introduction
Dialogue
Action / Reactions
Characteristics
Description – Imagery
Backstory
Creating a Three Dimensional Character
Showing vs. Telling
Writing for Children – Finding Age Appropriate Words
Resources
Your Assignment

Section Three Introduction

FICTION WRITING IS an amazing journey. You get to create something from nothing. You can build characters, lands, other worlds, other languages, other beings. It's almost magical. And, most importantly, you get to spark a child's imagination.

Characters are ultimately people, like you and me, and that's what makes readers connect with them. As people, your characters need to have human characteristics (aside from some science fiction characters) - they need to be 'real.'

When you think of people around you what do you see or remember that makes them distinct or makes them memorable?

When I was in my early twenties, my maternal aunt was in the hospital with kidney failure. Not having any children of her own, I was like a daughter to her. One particular day, I can't remember what procedure the hospital was doing, but from the hallway I heard a gut wrenching scream. I'll never forget that scream . . . never. This is a human feeling and memory.

Your characters need to have human qualities: fears, sadness, happiness, struggles, successes . . . get the idea? If they don't possess these qualities, your reader won't form a connection and won't bother reading your story.

In this section we'll focus on creating and building your protagonist.

As with your story's plot and conflict, there is a character arc. This arc is in the form of some type of growing or transformation. While it doesn't have to be drastic, it does need to be recognizable and significant.

One tip here is that you obviously can't start with a 'perfect' character. If your character has no flaws, there will be no room for growth.

Let's look at the protagonist from *Walking Through Walls*. His initial objective is to get rich. His plan is to get rich by taking from others. He's lazy, selfish, impatient, and lacks direction. He has a lot of room for growth!

Some characters may not need a 'moral fix.' They may be striving to achieve something like Tree-ear from *A Single Shard*. He was a 'bridge-dweller' orphan and considered the 'low of the low.' His goal was to become a master potter, not for fame or wealth, but because he loved it.

Developing an engaging character who is able to establish a connection with the reader is essential to your story. The characterization you develop will create a sense of realism for the reader. Although this realism may be temporary, it will establish a connection that will pull the reader through the story. The reader will be concerned about the protagonist and his journey – this is the reason developing a realistic character is essential.

Children want to recognize themselves in the protagonist, or an exaggerated version of themselves, especially in chapter books through young adult. They need to understand the character's dilemma or problem. They want and need to identify with the character.

According to CBI Publisher Laura Backes, in her article *Creating Believable Middle Grade and Young Adult Characters*, the middle grade and young adult reader also needs "the characters to be a bit bigger, braver, or smarter than themselves. The problems must be more dramatic than the readers' own, the stakes higher. Tension builds when protagonists act more impulsively, foolhardy or selfishly than the reader would ever do. Novels for older readers portray a magnified version of real life."

The same is true for the older picture-book-aged children. They want their "characters to be a bit bigger, braver, or smarter than themselves."

A good story and characterization will take the reader on a journey, one that she feels, one that she's a part of. And, an exceptional characterization will make the character memorable.

Think of some memorable protagonists, such as:

- Harry Potter
- Tally in *Uglies* by Scott Westerfeld
- The Cat in the Hat
- Winnie the Pooh
- Peter Pan
- Pocahontas
- Alice in Wonderland
- Dorothy in the *Wizard of Oz*
- Romeo and Juliette
- Scout in *To Kill a Mockingbird*
- Tom Sawyer
- Huckleberry Finn
- Shrek
- Scarlett in *Gone With The Wind*
- Hamlet
- James Bond
- Elizabeth Bennett in *Pride and Prejudice*
- Columbo and Monk – TV characters

All these characters made a connection, a bond with the reader through dialogue, along with their actions and reactions.

With all this in mind, you will need to create and build your character through a number of strategies, including:

- Dialogue
- Actions and reactions
- Characteristics
- Description – visual impressions
- Backstory

The focus will be primarily on dialogue, but we'll also cover the other strategies.

Dialogue

DIALOGUE IS ONE of the most significant character-building tools. Through dialogue, whether it's internal or external, you get a snapshot of who that character is, what makes him tick. And, it's a great 'showing' tool.

Before we go on, you'll need to understand what internal and external dialogue is.

Mary Kole, in her blog post titled "Interiority vs. Telling," explains interiority as being privy to "a character's thoughts, feelings, and reactions to the situation."

So, inner dialogue is the character's thoughts.

Let's start with how Wang's character, from *Walking Through Walls*, is conveyed through dialogue.

Within the conversation between Wang and his father, we're shown a bit of Wang's character:

"Wang, I am busy. The Eternals are a legend. Stop being so involved with magic. Occupy your time with more practical matters. You need to spend more time in the fields helping me." His father lifted his reaper hook, and went back to work.

According to this quote, Wang is known as being more of a dreamer than a doer or worker. It's a glimpse into his character. It's establishing his character base.

Another quote that helps covey Wang's character is in a conversation with the village mayor. Wang has asked him if he might know where the Eternals live:

The Mayor stared at the boy. "Wang, why do you want to know such a thing."

"I want to be become an Eternal."

The Mayor shook his head and laughed. "Wang, what are we to do with you? You are always scheming."

Here we have yet another facet of Wang's makeup. Notice how these bits of conversation unveil who Wang is. It's done subtly.

Another example of dialogue revealing a character's essence is from *Stephanie's Ponytail*, mentioned in Section One. Through simple dialogue Stephanie is shown to be her own person, wanting to be unique:

One day Stephanie went to her mom and said, "None of the kids in my class have a ponytail. I want a nice ponytail coming right out the back."

Stephanie proudly goes to school with her ponytail and the other kids tell her it's ugly. Her response:

"It's *my ponytail* and *I* like it."

This is all on the very first page. Stephanie has shown the reader that she is a leader, not a follower. Kids will easily identify with this. And, notice how the author italicized "my ponytail' and "I," adding emphasis to her individualism.

Now, let's go back to *Walking Through Walls*:

Lying on his bed, Wang opened the book to where he had left off. *Father thinks the Eternals are a myth. He thinks my goals are selfish and foolish. Wait. We will see how foolish Father is when I know magic and have great power. I will be the richest man in all of China. The sixteenth century will become the Wang period.*

This is from the first chapter and there are a few good observations we can make.

1. Internal thoughts are usually italicized. This allows for the young reader to quickly ascertain that the character is revealing his inner thoughts. And there isn't any dialogue punctuation when italicizing inner thoughts.

2. In one short paragraph we learn quite a bit: Wang is selfish, head strong, doesn't listen, and wants to get rich and have great power through magic. He has very lofty thoughts. And, you learn that his father doesn't approve of his intentions. This is character building through inner dialogue.

Here's another example of inner dialogue:

PLOP. Wang's hand grew limp, and the book fell to the floor. He opened his eyes and blinked. *Where is the dragon? It could not be a dream, or could it? The sensation of reigning over such a beast still pulsated in his blood. This is the power I want – controlling great forces.*

While there's a bit of prior text leading up to this quote, without using 'telling,' you now know that Wang 'felt' the power he wants – now he can visualize it, and so can you.

So, why is dialogue preferred over narration?

That question brings us to 'showing and telling.'

Showing lets the reader feel the protagonist's pain, or joy, or excitement. It conveys through action and dialogue, and that creates a connection and prompts the reader to continue reading.

Telling is flat, it's boring. It doesn't create the same connection showing does.

The difference is easier to see with an example. Using the same quote as above, I'll rewrite it using telling:

Lying on his bed, Wang opened the book to where he had left off. His father thought Wang was foolish, but Wang would show him. Once Wang learned the magic he needed, he'd be rich and powerful. Wang could envision himself being the richest man in all of China.

Can you see the difference?

The actual boxed quote created a connection with the reader. You saw Wang's inner thoughts - there was NO middle man. It is personal.

The latter rewritten text is telling. It's information being conveyed by the narrator. It isn't 'up close and personal,' there's a distance.

Telling is kind of like seeing someone standing on the other side of a stream. He's close enough to see what he's wearing, you can see his movement, you may even be able to talk to him, but there's a distance, or in the case of 'telling' an intangible obstacle between you.

To help create a deeper understanding of the difference between 'showing and telling' I'll use another example. This is from one of my blog posts:

An example of telling:

April walked around in a daze. She felt awful. Her husband left her with two little ones. She cried and cried. She felt overwhelmed, but kept doing the things she had to do. It seemed as if her soul ached. She begged for God's help. She felt like screaming.

An example of showing:

"He wasn't supposed to leave. We promised to stay married forever," April whispered. She pulled the sheets from the bed and threw them to the floor. Doing the chores and taking care of the kids helped her hold on. She seemed to be floating . . . outside of herself . . . she had to hold on. How could he leave?

Tears trickled down her cheeks. She bent forward with her head in her hands. "Please, God, bring him home . . . please . . . please help me." Sobbing softly in her hands her body began to tremble; then the tears gushed forth. An indescribable ache took hold - in the very depths of her soul - an ache in a place never felt before. A tortured scream crept up into her throat, ready to burst out. She fell to her knees and buried her face in the mattress. Grabbing a pillow, she pulled it over her head. A blood-curdling scream issued forth.

This should help you get the idea. You want to make the reader feel what the character is feeling. Telling just doesn't do that.

While there will be some telling necessary, as in descriptions and some information, you want to limit it. Show your story through action, dialogue, and sensory details.

It may help to draw from personal experiences to get the feeling and words you're going for. You can also use TV or movies; watch and study scenes that depict the experience you need to convey. Then, write what you've seen.

Showing is done through action, dialogue, and sensory detail (taste, touch, sight, sound, and smell).

From the article "Why do we Show, Don't Tell in our Writing?," multi-published (80+ books) children's author, Robyn Opie explains, "The most important thing that 'showing' does is to make us care. Why do we care? Because we're involved, we're participating. When we're involved and participating, then it matters to us. It makes a difference."

She goes on to note that 'telling' doesn't have this effect – it doesn't "engage the imagination." The narrator is simply telling the reader something. There is no thought process, no interpretation, no participation on the reader's part. The conclusion has been laid out. "We cannot see, hear, feel or think about the words. We're kept outside the story, at a distance. And we have no choice but to accept what the writer says as gospel."

With this said, dialogue should not be used as an 'information dump.' Here's an example of information dumping:

"What's the matter?" Beth asked. "I haven't seen you this droopy since Dad up and left in the middle of the night last year and we all had to try to figure out how to survive on Mom's bitty income waiting tables at the Awful Waffle."

"Yeah," Bobby said thoughtfully as he remembered those terrible days of questioning whether he was the reason Dad left. Dad never liked Bobby's interest in books and drawing instead of sports and hunting. "But this is even worse. There's a bully at school who is picking on me. You know how much shorter I am than all the other guys and how I can't seem to put on weight no matter how much I eat. Mom says I'm scrawny as a plucked chicken. How can I deal with a bully who is twice my size?"

Do you notice the dumping?

In the example dialogue, the characters are 'dumping' information purely for the reader's sake. This character backstory would already be known by the characters themselves. Be aware, kids are savvy and will pick up on this. It may very well push the reader away, rather than fostering an emotional connection.

Backstory, whether in dialogue or through the narrator, needs to be introduced in 'bits and pieces.'

Here's a bit more information on the topic:

Children's Writing and Information Dump
http://karencioffiwritingforchildren.com/2017/04/30/childrens-writing-information-dump/

This should give you a pretty good understanding of the importance of dialogue, how to use it to further characterization, and about showing rather than telling. But, I've included a couple of articles and links on 'showing and telling,' along with other relevant information for this Section at the end. You'll find it before the assignment.

Final note on dialogue: Make sure your story has age appropriate words, dialogue, and action.

Moving along, now we'll see how dialogue can further develop your character.

Actions and Reactions

ACTIONS AND REACTIONS is another 'biggie' in developing a realistic and engaging character. As with dialogue, it creates a connection with the reader. It might be the reader will see herself in the character, see someone she would love to be, see someone she hates, or see someone who might be her friend. All this lends itself to reader involvement.

So, how do actions and reactions demonstrate facets of a character and move that character forward?

Both actions and reactions can be shown through physical movement, expressions, emotions, dialogue, and the senses. And, as with dialogue, it brings us deeper into the character. Each action gives us a glimpse of another facet of the character.

Let's use some examples to demonstrate this.

From Stephanie's Ponytail:

After Stephanie proudly told her class that she didn't care if they [her class-mates] thought her ponytail was ugly, the very next day all the girls wore ponytails coming right out the back of their heads. So, the next day, Stephanie decided on another unique ponytail:

"Stephanie would you like a ponytail coming out the back?"

Stephanie said, "No."

"Then that's that," said her mom. "That's the only place you can do ponytails."

"No, it's not," said Stephanie. "I want one coming out the side, just above my ear."

You have to love this character. Her reaction to the class copying her was to find another means of individuality – she got angry that she was copied. In her response or action to this new obstacle it shows she's determined and clever. This further builds her character.

Now back to *Walking Through Walls:*

Wang managed to get the formula to one magic feat from the Master Eternal and is learning how to make it work. The Master tells Wang that he can never say the words to the formula out loud or even in a whisper.

"Uh," he paused, "Master what will happen if I do say the words to the magic formula out loud?"

"Wang, you are trying to delay your task. It is a good question, though. Your tongue will cease its movement . . ."

Wang's eyes opened wide as he flung his hands on top of his head. *Never to talk again! I am sorry I asked for the formula. What if I slip?*

This quote gives us a couple of extra details into Wang's personality:

1. The task at hand is frightening and he's again trying to get out of something he doesn't want to do.

2. He has a particular habit of throwing his hands up or on top of his head when he's flabbergasted. This trait has been weaved throughout the story.

3. He can be unknowingly funny: "What if I slip?"

Next, we'll go on to characteristics.

Characteristics

CHARACTERIZATION IS ALL in the details. According to author/poet Maggie Ball, "you need details, specifics, visual impressions, motion."

Characteristics can be demonstrated in a number of ways:

It can be a particular way the character speaks – maybe words he favors.

It can be in mannerisms or gestures. I gave a hint of this in #2 of the details in the last quote: Wang has the habit of throwing his hands up in the air or on top of his head when he's flabbergasted. Maybe a character chews gum all the time, or bites his nails, or has a smoking habit.

It can be in their physical characteristics:

Stephanie's hair is long enough to put into a ponytail.

Crane-man, from *A Single Shard,* is one-legged from birth, and walks with a crutch.

Superman is faster than a speeding bullet, able to leap tall buildings in a single bound, more powerful than a locomotive.

It can be in their innate qualities:

Tree-ear is meek and respectful.
Harry Potter is a genius and a wizard.
Winn-Dixie (the dog) could actually smile.
Batman is a genius.

It can be in their occupation, personal or family status

Opal's father is a preacher.
Tree-ear is an orphan and considered in the lowest of statuses.
Popeye is a sailor and gets extra strength from eating spinach.
Clark Kent is a mild-mannered reporter and was an orphan.

It can be in their personality, acquired or developed:

Wang doesn't like hard work and lacks patience.
Stephanie likes to be unique, is determined, and smart.
Winnie the Pooh loves honey and he'll do just about anything to get it.
Bugs Bunny is conniving and clever.
Batman is somber.

I know some of these examples are silly, but I think they help convey what characteristics are. Characteristics help build and strengthen your character and the bond he'll develop with the readers.

One strategy to help build your character is to use character sheets.

CHARACTER SHEETS: Adding Dimension to Your Protagonist

Connecting with a reader entails a couple of things, one of which is to have a fully developed protagonist. A crucial aspect of creating a 'real' character is his interactions with the other characters in the story, and his reactions to external influences. These reactions to external surroundings or occurrences add layers to your protagonist.

To be able to write with this type of clarity and dimension for your protagonist, you need to know every detail of your protagonist's character. Even if you learn tidbits here and there as the story progresses, the new bits and pieces of the characters traits will need to be remembered and possibly used again.

An example of knowing your character is Chapter Five of *Walking Through Walls*. It's the second day of his 'work' training and Wang drops his axe on his foot. After screaming and sitting in pain, he waits to see if another student will come to his aid. No one does. Notice how he reacts:

He hobbled over to the closest student. "Excuse me. Did you not see what happened? I could have used some help."

The student threw his axe over his shoulder. "Yes, I saw. However, every student is expected to take care of himself. We cannot offer assistance."

Wang shook his head. He hobbled and hopped back to his spot, picked up his axe, and went back to chopping wood. *They cannot help? What if I did cut off my foot? What then?*

Here we have a bit of sarcasm on Wang's part. I know this about him so wrote his reaction to demonstrate it. But, as an author, you will need to keep track of new facets or existing facets of a character's personality or being.

An excellent way to keep track of your protagonist's characteristics is to create a character sheet.

Using Character Sheets

Make note on your character sheet of every reaction and interaction your character has with another character. As with actual life, we interact differently with different people in our lives. A boy will not react to a friend the same way he does a brother. He will not react the same to a sister as he does a brother.

The same holds true for all other relationships. All these different interactions help create a fully dimensional protagonist.

As you're creating your story's characters' dynamics, keep in mind that all characters play a part in creating a realistic story, even in fantasy and sci-fi. What this means is that your protagonist needs a responsive partner or team member (character) when interacting, otherwise the interaction will feel one-sided and flat.

Create Character Continuity

In order to create a continuity of character traits for all characters, each character needs a character sheet. While for some this may seem tedious, it is well worth the effort. You may be three quarters through the manuscript and can't remember how character A interacted with character D. You won't want to have to search through the story to find this little tidbit of information.

A second strategy you can use to help develop your characters is doing a character interview. It may sound silly, but it can work wonders. Do it the same way you'd interview a 'real' person.

CHARACTER INTEVIEW

As you ask questions, you'll need to come up with answers, thus developing your character.

Your character interview should, or may, include:

Name, age, family, history, place of birth, where he lives, friends, social status, etc.
Physical attributes: color of hair, eyes, any impairments, tall, short, etc.
Idiosyncrasies: washes his hands a lot, won't eat red foods, etc.
Mannerisms: shrugs a lot, blinks too much, laughs too loud, scratches his head, etc.
Innate qualities: smart, kind, mean, tough, happy, sad, friendly, stand-offish, etc.

Hobbies/sports: likes puzzles, likes baseball, hates basketball, etc.

Habits: chews gum, taps his foot, leaves the milk container on the counter, etc.

Personal preferences: he's not crazy about school, he hates math, he loves science

Does he have a girlfriend, a past romantic history?

Did he suffer any accidents as a child?

Did he suffer through any tragedies?

Is he bullied or a bully?

Make a template of specific questions and answers that you think are pertinent to developing your character. Add as many questions and answers as you can come up with. Some interview templates are very comprehensive, even including religion.

W. Somerset Maugham said, "You can never know enough about your characters."

Also, keep in mind that **each character will have his/her own motivation for actions and reactions.** This is part of their character traits, as well as the story's plot, and should be listed on their character sheet. Readers love characters who are worth reading about – they love characters who are funny, courageous, intelligent . . . characters who create that 'special' connection.

Remember, every action, reaction, and interaction created in your story will not only develop the protagonist, but also the other characters in the story.

I'll have more information, links or articles at the end of the Section to provide additional reading and insight into creating characteristics.

Next up is Description – Imagery.

Description - Imagery

Probably one of the most difficult aspects of writing is providing content that your reader can turn into pictures or imagery. You may know exactly what you're trying to convey, the image you want your reader to see, but does your content (your text) translate into effective imagery for your reader? Does your description work?

Stephen King discusses this topic in an informative article in the August 2010 *The* Writer magazine. Obviously, any advice from this author is valuable, but I especially like his views on imagery. **A key tip that struck me is**: "Imagery does not occur on the writer's page; it occurs in the reader's mind."

The question that follows is: how does a writer transfer what's in her mind into the mind of the reader?

The answer is through description.

Unfortunately, it's not as easy as it sounds. What many writers may tend to do is offer too many details that aren't necessary and may weigh the story down. According to King, you need to pick and choose the most important details and descriptions that will allow the reader to understand what you're conveying, but also provide enough room for the reader to create her own unique image.

To accomplish this task, King says to "leave in details that impress you the most strongly: leave in the details you see the most clearly; leave everything else out."

The strategy in this is to look carefully at what you want to convey. Picture an image in your mind and focus on the key aspects, the aspects that give you a clear picture of what it is. Then, write what you see. Again, this may not be easy to do, but King suggests that there is another vision tool to use, which he calls "a third eye" of imagination and memory.

What we see is translated to our brain. Once there we need to interpret that image and transcribe it into content that will provide the reader with a strong gist of what it is, but also allow the reader to fill in her own details. And, those details should convey what you're targeting.

For example: *The house stood dark and dreary.*

While this simple sentence provides imagery that should enable the reader to create a picture, there are probably not enough details for the basic image you might be going for. What color is the house? Is it in disrepair? Is it a new or old house, big or small?

A possible alternative to the above example that adds a little more detail, but not too much, is: *Cracked shingles hung on the dingy grey house; chipped paint and missing caulking on the windows further emphasized its disrepair.*

Another example of description is from *Walking Through Walls*:

Wang bound the last bunch of wheat stalks as the sun beat down on the field. Sweat poured from the back of his neck drenching the cotton shirt he wore.

The two sentences provide sufficient imagery for the reader to understand the situation, while not giving too many details. If you notice, the content doesn't mention the color of his shirt, or if Wang kneeled on the ground or hunched over the bundle. It's also missing a number of other details that aren't necessary and would weigh the story down.

Interestingly, along with concise details, your characters' names might also add imagery to your story. When you read my character's name, Wang, what image comes to mind?

The next description example below is from *The Lucky Baseball: My Story in a Japanese-American Internment Camp*:

After dinner we went to find the latrines. We didn't have to look too hard. We could smell them before we saw them. There were separate latrines for the men and women. I didn't go in the women's latrine, of course, but the men's latrine was disgusting. It was a big room with toilet bowls lined up back-to-back in the middle of the floor and a line of showers behind them. The plumbing was not working properly and most of the toilets were either overflowing or filled to the brim. I decided that the shrubs behind the latrine would be my toilet most of the time from now on.

In this historical middle grade novel, the author wanted to convey what it was like being in an internment camp during WWII. She did an excellent job. In the scene, she also described the barracks. This story is a great example of bringing history to life and having a reader absorbed in a story.

You might think of your story's imagery as an outline or sketch, rather than a colored and finely detailed painting. The basic idea is there for your reader to enhance with her own imagination and memory.

Now on to Backstory.

Backstory

IF WE DIDN'T know Batman's backstory – his parents were both murdered in front him when he was a young boy – would we be sympathetic to his somber personality, or understand his drive to fight evil?

If we didn't know what happened to Snow White, would we be sympathetic toward her sleeping 'problem?'

If we didn't know Harry Potter's parents were both dead, would we have the same vision or interpretation of what was going on in the story?

The trauma, the emotion-wrenching hurt that a character goes through allows for sympathy, understanding, and a connection with the reader. This backstory also provides the 'motive' for the character's actions and goals.

Backstory, though, doesn't need to be about severe trauma. It could be a set-up of the character's traits, why he does certain things, the motivation behind his actions.

You do need to be careful when adding backstory – you don't want to tear the reader from the momentum of your story. Backstory needs to be added in' bits and pieces.' And, it's helpful if it's casually brought up in character conversations, or brief descriptions.

Using *A Single Shard* and then *Walking Through Walls* as examples we'll look into backstory.

Tree-ear did an honest deed for a farmer and is rewarded for it:

Tree-ear had learned from Crane-man's example. Foraging in the woods and rubbish heaps, gathering fallen grain-heads in the autumn – these were honorable ways to garner a meal, requiring time and work. But, stealing and begging, Crane-man said, made a man no better than a dog.

"Work gives a man dignity, stealing takes it away," he said.

This is a great example of backstory. You learn:

Crane-man is and has always been honest and a hard worker.

The pair of bridge-dwellers are poor.

Tree-ear gets his moral substance from Crane-man.

Crane-man is Tree-ear's mentor or guardian.

If the story hadn't already let you know, you'd surmise that Crane-man and Tree-ear lived together for a long while.

Notice that this backstory isn't cumbersome. It conveys what it must and that's it. This story has many such backstory 'stops' deepening the reader's experience and understanding of why some things were as they were, and giving more breadth and depth to the characters.

Now let's look at a bit of backstory from *Walking Through Walls*.

Wang finally found the Eternals and became an apprentice. He had a roommate, Chen, and assumed Chen became an apprentice for selfish reasons also.

Chen explained that he came to be an apprentice because his village sent him – they were counting on him:

"Counting on you for what?"

Chen lowered his head. "My village is in trouble. Powerful warriors raid our village and other villages whenever they need or want something. They took my sister, Yin, two months ago. She is just ten-years-old."

"That is horrid," whispered Wang, "my sister, SuLin, is the same age."

Now the reader has the backstory on Chen and it wasn't 'dumping' because Wang asked the question, he had no idea what the answer would be.

A character must have a motive for his actions. Otherwise, the character's actions are pointless and uninteresting. Chen needed to save his sister and the village. Wang desired to be rich and powerful through magic.

The character needs to overcome any obstacles that get in the way of his goals. And, overcoming those obstacles will help define his true nature and transform him.

In children's writing, this transformation must be a direct result of the trials and tribulations he goes through to overcome those obstacles.

In writing for young children, such as picture books for the younger age group, backstory should be avoided. When writing for the young child the timeframe should be current and the story itself should be told within a short period of time – a few hours, a day, or a couple of days.

Remember, the young child doesn't have the same reference or understanding of time.

Also, children's picture books are usually well under 1000 words. This calls for tight writing. There's NO room for backstory.

Creating a Three-Dimensional Character

BETWEEN YOUR CHARACTERS, the plot, and the other writing elements, you develop a story. If the mix is right, and the characters are believable, you can create a story worthy of publication.

Creating believable characters is an essential part of writing, and they need to be as life-like as possible. To accomplish this, you need to have a three-dimensional protagonist.

So, which is your protagonist?

Is your protagonist flat - lacks any type of emotion and action, like the simple and safe kiddy rides at a children's amusement park, the carousel horse that goes round and round, but does nothing else? If so, then you have a one dimensional character on your hands.

Is your protagonist a little bumpy - he has some quirks, life and emotion, but no real depth of character or history, like the carousel horse that goes round and round and up and down at a steady easy pace? Then you have a two dimensional character struggling to break into the world of believability.

Is your protagonist a full blown amusement park - a roller coaster, full of ups and downs, knowledge, emotion, character, quirks, life, flaws, and history? Now you have it; you have a believable three dimensional character that is strong enough to bring your story through to the end.

There will also be times when your character tells you who he is:

"The moment comes when a character does or says something you hadn't thought about. At that moment he's alive and you leave it to him."

~ Graham Greene

Showing vs. Telling

THE SECRET TO showing is to pay attention and it gets easier with practice and time.

When looking at a sentence, really examine it. Did you tell the reader what happened or did you show him through dialogue or the characters' actions/senses?

Here's a simple example:

John was tired and wished he was home already. (TELLING)

John's shoulders drooped. He slouched forward with his head hung low. He dug his hands deep into his pockets. He just wanted to get home. (SHOWING)

The problem with 'showing,' is that it can sometimes use more words. So, you might cut "slouched forward" and "his hands dug deep into his pockets."

John's shoulders drooped and his head hung low.

You can also create 'showing' by using dialogue - this is a good trick when you can't come up with an action scene or find the right words:

John's shoulders drooped. "Man, I wish I was home already. What a rough day."

Another example:

John's book bag was so heavy it kept falling off his shoulder. (TELLING)

John jerked his shoulder, putting his book bag back in place. "If they give me one more book to take home, I'm goin' on strike." (SHOWING)

John tugged at the book bag on his shoulder. "Why don't they just give us bricks to carry." (SHOWING)

Sometimes it helps to think of a character you've seen on TV or the movies who was in a similar situation as your character. How was he standing? Where were his hands? What was his body doing? What were his facial expressions?

If you're really stuck, you might try to act it out. Would your eyes be darting, fixated on an object, looking up, down . . .

Another trick is to catch all the sentences you have "was" in. The word WAS is a weak verb. Once you find them, see if you can rewrite the sentence eliminating the weak verb. Just be sure the clarity of the sentence remains intact.

Also watch for the overuse of adjectives, such as "ly" words: quickly, speedily.

An example: She quickly zoomed across the room.
(Zoomed infers speed – adding 'quickly' to the sentence is overkill and an overuse of adjectives.)

Another example of the overuse of adjectives:

It was a *bright, sunny* day.
(Using either bright or sunny would be sufficient. And, if you're writing an under 1000-word picture book, it would add needlessly to the word count.)

You can use your FIND function in Word to catch WAS words and LY words.

In addition, **watch for the overuse of adverbs.**
Here's an example of the overuse of adverbs:

Not correct: The girl ran really super-fast to catch up with her friends.
Correct: The girl raced to catch up with her friends.

Writing for Children: Finding Age Appropriate Words

WRITING IN GENERAL can be a tough business; writing for children is even tougher.

Writing for children has its own unique tricks, processes, and rules; one of those rules is using words that are age appropriate.

How this differs from writing in general is that the children's writing arena is divided into specific age groups. **The question is**: How does a writer know which words are specific to a particular age group?

Unless you are an experienced writer and have become very familiar with the different age group vocabularies, you will need help in this area.

One particular source/tool for finding age appropriate words IS the *Children's Writers Word Book*, 2nd Edition, by Alijandra Mogilner and Tayopa Mogilner.

This book lists specific words that are introduced at seven key reading levels (kindergarten through sixth grade). It provides a thesaurus of those words with synonyms, annotated with reading levels. In addition, it offers detailed guidelines for sentence length, word usage, and themes at each reading level. I find it a valuable tool in my writing toolbelt.

There are also other books and sites available that will help you in your search for those age appropriate words for your children's book, just do an online search.

Section Three Resources

HERE ARE LINKS to a number of excellent articles relevant to this Section:

How to Show Not Tell
http://writetodone.com/2011/11/28/john-lecarre-show-not-tell/

Understanding Showing and Telling
http://www.advancedfictionwriting.com/blog/2010/08/26/understanding-showing-and-telling/

How to Create Realistic Characters
http://inkpop.wordpress.com/2010/03/11/how-to-create-realistic-characters/

All Characters Aren't Created Equal
http://seekerville.blogspot.com/2011/07/all-characters-arent-created-equalguest.html

Plot a Lesson from Aristotle about Building Characters
http://educationwantstobefree.blogspot.com/2011/09/lesson-from-aristotle-about-building.html

List of Character Traits
http://character-in-action.com/list-of-character-traits/

Describing characters with Similes
http://www.jillmcdougall.com.au/content/view/127/32/

Plot and Your Story – Four Formats
http://karencioffiwritingforchildren.com/2015/10/19plot-and-your-story-four-formats/

Flashing Back
http://gailcarsonlevine.blogspot.com/2010/05/flashing-back.html

Villains
http://mysterywritingismurder.blogspot.com/2012/03/villainsby-joan-swan.html

Character Self-Description
http://kidlit.com/2011/10/24/character-self-description/

Seven Character Types That Build Your Story
http://childrenspublishing.blogspot.com/2011/10/seven-character-types-that-build-your.html

Creating Characters
http://www.writersonthemove.com/2011/10/creating-characters.html

Three Character Archetypes in Fiction
http://www.helpingwritersbecomeauthors.com/three-character-archetypes-in-fiction/

All Characters Aren't Created Equal
http://seekerville.blogspot.com/2011/07/all-characters-arent-created-equalguest.html

Physical Clichés
http://kidlit.com/2011/06/01/physical-cliches/

An Observation On Character Development
http://pubrants.blogspot.com/2011/09/observation-on-character-development.html

Putting the Character into Characterization
http://storyfix.com/putting-the-character-into-characterization

Crafting Authentic Dialogue
http://www.novelpublicity.com/2010/12/the-wordy-transition-crafting-authentic-dialogue/

The 7 Tools of Dialogue
http://www.writersdigest.com//article/?p_ArticleId=28051

For those who purchased the book in paperback, for clickable links go to:
http://karencioffiwritingforchildren.com/writing-fiction-for-children-articles/

Section Three Assignment

- - - - - - - - - - - - - - -

In SECTION TWO, your assignment was to create a one page beginning. This one page should have introduced your protagonist.

You can continue on with your first page for the rest of the sections.

1. For Section Three, you will create one or two more characters, one being the antagonist, if your story's conflict is caused by a character.

What I mean here is that in *Walking Through Walls*, a character wasn't the antagonist, the conflict came from Wang's own desires and his struggles to reach them – it was an internal conflict.

2. Create character sheets for each of your characters, including the protagonist:

Include the characters' basics: Name, age, gender, physical attributes, and main characteristics. If you know them at this point, include each characters' motives and the stakes involved for not reaching their goals.

You'll be adding to these sheets as you write your story and as your characters add new elements to their personas.

3. Prepare a basic character interview for each character. Use the information in Characteristics: Character Interview (around page 54).

You might also think about what makes your character engaging. Why would a reader care about him? Will the reader learn anything from him? And, how do your characters differ?

Section
Four

Fundamentals and Strengthening the Middle

THE MIDDLE OF your story builds momentum, suspense, and reader involvement. It moves forward to the climax of the story. This section will show you how to build and strengthen your middle to carry the reader to her final destination: THE END.

It will also include some additional story fundamentals, including conflict.

Section Four Content:
Introduction: Writing a Story
Story Fundamentals
Strengthening the Middle
Looking at Examples
Upping the Stakes Ups the Tension / Antagonist / Subplots
Balance in Writing: The Major Elements
What Makes a Good Story: Plot Driven or Character Driven?
Theme and Your Story
Resources
Your Assignment

Writing a Story

JOINING THE STORY together in a seamless fashion is probably the trickiest part of writing. The characters, conflict, plot, theme, setting, and other details all need to blend together to create something grander than their individual parts, like the ingredients of a cake. This is called synergy.

It doesn't matter if your story is plot driven or character driven, all the elements need to weave together smoothly to create the desired affect you are going for: humor, mystery, action, fantasy, suspense, or other.

If you have an action packed plot driven story, but it lacks believable and sympathetic characters, you're story will be lacking. The same holds true if you have a believable and sympathetic character but the story lacks movement. It will also usually fall short.

All this must be done in an engaging manner along with easy to understand content.

With that said, let's get into Lesson Four.

When writing your story, think of an arc.

Your story begins at the bottom and slowly rises to the peak of the arc and then comes down the other side toward the ending.

The up side of your arc will have your protagonist struggling through the obstacles that prevent him from reaching his goals

You might also think of the story arc as stepping stones, each bringing your protagonist closer to success and the reader closer to a satisfying ending.

Keep in mind though that the story arc doesn't have to be even on both sides – many arcs have a slow steady upward movement through two-third or three-quarters of the arc, then come down the other side enlightening the reader as to how the protagonist overcame that final obstacle and transformed himself.

But, before we get into building and strengthening the middle of your story, let's look at a couple of story fundamentals.

One last tidbit of information here: writing is an art form, therefore rules for one writer may not work another. And, different stories may call for a somewhat different structure. There are however some basic guidelines to writing a story that many writers adhere to.

Story Fundamentals

YOUR STORY BEGINS with an idea, whether it's your own, from a folktale, or other. As mentioned in the previous section, you may opt to write an outline for your story, guiding you along. Or, you may opt for the seat-of-the-pants method. Note though that the outline does provide some security and guidance.

There are two components that allow a story to be built:

Story structure: According to <u>Larry Brooks</u>, "story structure is the sequence of your scenes that result in a story well written" (*Story Engineering*, 138).

Story architecture: "Story architecture is the empowerment of those scenes through compelling characterizations, powerful thematic intentions, a fresh and intriguing conceptual engine, and a writing voice that brings it all to life with personality and energy" (138).

If you like we can compare this to a house or car.

The structure of a house is its foundation, the beams, floors, and roof that work together to hold it up and together. If it were a car, it would be the chassis. It is the skeleton, the framework.

The architecture of a house would be the floor plans, design, and furnishings. In a car, it would be everything built upon the chassis. It's the substance to the entity. It's what gives it personality.

Having a father who built houses and then went into auto mechanics, I can relate to these analogies, I hope you can also.

So, this is the bear-bottom fundamentals of story writing. "Structure is craft. Architecture is art," as <u>Brooks</u> aptly puts it (138).

Before you begin your story, think of it as an empty vessel, kind of like a container. In it you will put your characters, plot, theme, setting, subplot, conflict, and so on – all the elements of a story. But, just having them in the container won't do much for a coherent and engaging story that will have readers turning the pages. NO, it won't. You will need to arrange those elements in a way that grabs the reader and keeps her reading.

As a house has rooms in which to decorate and furnish, a story has four levels or parts in which you will put the story elements.

Level One is the Setup.

We went over this in Section Two. Your setup has a grabbing beginning and hints at the trouble ahead for the protagonist. It provides the inciting incident. Its sole objective is to establish the stakes involved, thus setting up the plot.

If Chen, in *Walking Through Walls*, was the protagonist of the story, the stakes would be the safety of his sister and village. The more serious the stakes, the stronger the emotion that's summoned. And it's emotion that keeps readers reading.

Although, the stakes don't have to be life or death, they could be finding true love, finding happiness, overcoming an addiction, overcoming serious health problems, overcoming being bullied, dealing with a family move, and so on. The stakes could be anything that might happen in real life.

Level One of a story also usually introduces the conflict. Without conflict you cannot have a story. A story without conflict would be like a car without an engine. It just wouldn't work.

Think of conflict as the obstacle in the protagonist's path. It's stopping him from reaching his goal, so he must overcome it. Maybe he'll go around it. Maybe he'll go over it. Maybe he'll dig under it and pass by that way. Maybe he'll get a stick of dynamite and blast it to smithereens. You get the idea. It's your imagination that will create the means for the protagonist to overcome his obstacles.

Level Two is the protagonist's Response.

In Level One, you established the setup, what's at stake, the conflict, or potential conflict. Level Two, like a building block on top of Part One, shows the protagonist's responses to the conflict and/or his nemesis.

Every action on the protagonist's part in this level is a response to the conflict. He might be considered a victim in this level.

The response may be, like in Chen's case, striving to learn something in order to have the necessary knowledge or power to overcome the conflict. It might be simply running from the conflict. It might also be an investigation to solve the conflict. It can be any engaging response, and the response/s will be throughout Level Two.

An example of this might be bullying. The protagonist is bullied – this would be introduced in Level One, the setup. Level Two will have him either hiding from the bully or learning ways to overcome the bully. These are responses to the conflict.

Level Two provides the protagonist with his purpose. It breathes life into him. It provides the motive for his quest.

Level Three is the Attack.

This is the part of the story in which the protagonist takes focus and begins to attack his obstacles. Rather than remaining fearful and in submission to his obstacle/s, he becomes emboldened and proactive. Maybe he gets angry. Maybe he's learned what he needed to and is now equipped to fight back. Maybe it's come down to 'do or die.'

Level Three will have the protagonist coming up with solutions in his attempts to fight back – some may work and others won't. It will be an uphill battle overcoming multiple obstacles. *This creates tension in the story and thickens the plot.*

A note here: let your protagonist win a couple of the minor battles during this level. It will keep the reader happy.

At the end of Level Three, a change comes about. Everything the protagonist needs to succeed is known or acquired. The pieces come together for the protagonist, putting him in the position to move onto Level Four.

Level Four is the Resolution.

This is the part of the story where the protagonist triumphs. He has grown or learned enough to take on the obstacles full force and prevail. Remember, for effective children's writing there must be some form of growth or transformation on the part of the protagonist.

"The hero [protagonist] needs to be the primary catalyst in the resolution of the story. The hero needs to be heroic" (*Story Engineering*, 156).

This is essential for children's writing. Even in the younger age groups, children must run the show. While you may have adults here and there in the story, it is the child protagonist who goes through the four levels of the story and comes up with the solution/s to his problem/s.

Level Four brings it all together, all loose ends are tied up, all questions are answered, the protagonist triumphs, and the reader is left satisfied.

While not all stories will be able to fall exactly into this basic writing structure, the majority will. When writing for young children it's a good idea to have around three obstacles that the protagonist overcomes one at a time.

A simple view of plotting your story is:

1. Something happens to the protagonist or he perceives something is wrong.
2. This leads him to respond by figuring a way out, because there are stakes involved.
3. He has a goal and takes action on his plan.
4. Someone or something puts a roadblock up.
5. The protagonist pushes through the roadblock.
6. There's another roadblock that he must overcome.
7. He struggles harder to overcome it, there is even more at stake.
8. There is yet another obstacle to overcome.
9. The protagonist learns something or grows in some way and is able to overcome the final obstacle and reach his goal.
10. This creates a satisfying ending.

As we go through the section, you'll see how this actually pans out.

Strengthening the Middle

USING THE FOUR levels of a story, your middle might consist of parts two and three. The protagonist responds to the obstacle or conflict and your reader watches, maybe putting in her two cents, "Don't run, fight!" Or, the reader may feel vested in how the protagonist reacts, 'will he or won't he.' At this point you're building tension and conflict. And, the protagonist is fighting back.

While you may have an interesting, funny, or mischievous protagonist who will keep the reader engaged, it most likely won't be enough to keep the reader turning the pages to the end? Conflict is needed for this.

It's conflict that will pull the reader through to the end of the story. The protagonist needs something to strive for or to overcome in order for the reader to remain engaged. This provides the element of growth within the story and it allows the reader to care and want to know what the outcome will be.

A story's conflict is like a detour or obstacle in the road from point A to point B. The protagonist must figure out a way over, around, under it, or through it. Getting past the obstacles in his path will help him to grow and mold his character.

A useful strategy that will help you create and build conflict is to use the 'how' and 'what if' questions to generate a spark. That spark will provide the conflict foundation. Then when one conflict is overcome, you can ask another 'how' or 'what if' question. This will get your story off and running, and flowing to the end.

Below are a couple of examples of scenarios and conflict questions:

Tommy wants more than anything to play baseball, but he's not very good. The other boys never willingly choose him for their team. How will Tommy overcome this problem?

What if Tommy gets the best bat and glove on the market—will this make him a better ball player?

Tommy gets the new bat and glove, but still can't play very well. What if he practices every day?

~~~~~

Kristen's friends all have new bikes, but she has her older sister's hand-me-down. Kristen needs to figure out a way to get a new bike, but how?

What if Kristen does extra chores around the house and earns the money?

What if Kristen finally gets a new bike and leaves it unattended at the park. It gets stolen. She's afraid to tell her parents, so keeps this little bit of information to herself. Does she feel guilty about lying? What if her little brother finds out and tells on her?

In the article "What to Aim For When Writing," Margot Finke advises, "A slow buildup of tension gives good pace. Dropping hints and clues builds tension, which in turn moves your story along. Short, punchy sentences give better pace than longwinded lines."

For chapter books, middle grade, and young adult, Finke advises to keep the reader engaged by ending each paragraph with a 'kind of' cliff-hanger. This doesn't mean you need a life and death scenario, just something that entices the reader to move onto the next chapter to find out what happens. In addition, to increase your story's pace in certain sections you can use shorter chapters of five to seven pages – this creates the sense of a quicker pace.

Short sentences, short paragraphs, and short chapters all have the tendency to quicken the story's pace and/or add tension.

Looking at Examples

LET'S START WITH *STEPHANIE'S PONYTAIL* for a simple example of conflict.

Stephanie is an individual. She wants to be distinct, unique. Each day, starting with her first ponytail "coming right out the back" she is confronted with an obstacle.

Day one, the kids in her class make fun of her and say her ponytail is ugly. This however doesn't waiver Stephanie. She simply tells the kids, "It's *my ponytail* and *I* like it." This establishes her leader qualities.

When Stephanie goes to school the next day, all the girls are wearing "ponytails coming out the back." This makes her angry and she calls them "copycats." But it also creates a dilemma for Stephanie. If all the girls are wearing ponytails just like her, how can she be unique?

Well, the next day she asks her mom to put her ponytail on the side of her head. This will teach those kids a lesson. At school, the kids tell her it's ugly. Stephanie doesn't care though, "It's *my ponytail* and *I* like it."

The next day, all the girls, and even some boys have a ponytail "coming out just above their ear." Again, this makes Stephanie angry. So, the next morning, she has her mom put the ponytail on top of her head, "like a tree." At school she's made fun of, but she doesn't care. "It's *my ponytail* and *I* like it."

What do you think happens the next day?

Yep, all the kids at school have a ponytail right on top of their heads. The next day she wears a ponytail cascading down her face. The next day the entire school have ponytails cascading down their faces.

At this point Stephanie has had it. Fuming, she screams, "When I come tomorrow, I am going to have . . . SHAVED MY HEAD!"

Now remember, Stephanie is smart. Do you think she shaved her head? What do you think the other kids did?

Do you see how in this simple story the tension grew. Each day Stephanie was faced with an obstacle and got angry, but she also overcame each obstacle. And, then, in Level Four of the story, she prevailed, outsmarting her classmates.

Each day consisted of a new scene in the story.

Raymond Obstfeld describes a scene as "the action that takes place in a single physical setting" (*Crafting Scenes*, 2). It can also be a focused concept or purpose or event in the story. We'll discuss scenes a bit further along in this section.

As a side note, *Stephanie's Ponytail* is an excellent example of repetition in children's writing. This technique is used in writing for younger children, the picture book ages. Children love to know what's coming next – it's like a game. You can picture the readers in a classroom or at home shouting out what Stephanie's class will do the next day.

Another great story that shows this desired repetition is *Caps for Sale* by Esphyr Slobodkina. If you're thinking of writing picture books, get your own copy of these books and study them carefully.

To strengthen your middle you need to add layers of new obstacles and information to overcome those obstacles, and develop the protagonist. You need to have the protagonist fight the uphill battle.

**Thelma and Louise** **is another example of building and strengthening your middle.**

While _Thelma and Louise_ isn't a book, movies have the same kind of structures as books. They have a beginning (the setup), the middle (response and attack), and the resolution.

The inciting incident in Thelma and Louise is when they shoot the man in the parking lot. At this point they had a choice: turn themselves in or run. Running changed their lives forever and caused an avalanche of tension-building events/scenes, strengthening its middle. This brings them into Level Two of the story – responding to the conflict by running.

To go back to 'scenes,' the parking lot would be one scene; back in the bar discussing what to do would be another scene. Each scene is dependent on the scene before. And, each scene should further the story along, building tension and/or suspense, providing more information, further developing the characters, or a combination of elements. And a scene can be one paragraph, two, three, or an entire chapter.

DISSECTING _WALKING THROUGH WALLS_

Wang is a typical child hero (protagonist). He's rebellious and headstrong, lazy like some teens, and fights with his sister, but the ancient Chinese setting gives him more liberties than a contemporary child would have.

The setting allows for Wang to journey off on his own, even at twelve. So, when writing a story keep in mind that all the elements of a story will lend themselves to making a story what it is.

CHAPTER ONE

Looking at *Walking Through Walls,* the inciting incident and catalyst for Wang's journey happened in the first chapter. Wang had a dream of riding on a powerful dragon that he had control over. This is the scene that motivated him to change his life:

This is the power I want – controlling great forces. He sat up and examined the room; with a crinkled brow his eyes strained to see what was not there. *Could the legend be true? Could the Eternals be summoning me?* Inspired by the dream, Wang knew he must find the Eternals. His thirst for knowledge became a powerful desire to go on an unforgettable journey.

CHAPTER TWO

The dream sends Wang on his quest to find the Eternals and lays the groundwork for the following scenes. In chapter two, he asks everyone he knows if they could tell him where to find the Eternals. He is driven and finally gets the information haphazardly from his little sister. Each scene furthers the story along.

CHAPTER THREE

Not caring that his family doesn't want him to go, or that he's needed at home to help his father, Wang goes off to where the Eternals live.

"Wang, I am asking you to stay here. Do not go."

"Father, I am sorry, but I must travel this path." He stepped back and gazed at his family for a moment. Lowering his eyes, he turned and took the first step toward a magical world.

This is the end of chapter three and further develops Wang's character and moves the story along to him journeying to the Loa Mountain.

Also, this brings up two important points about developing your character, tension building and strengthening your middle. Notice the last quoted paragraph.

While Wang is going to leave, before he actually leaves he gazes at his family and looks down. **Right here, the protagonist connects with the reader.** Prior to this, Wang is completely self-centered. This one scene shows a 'heartfelt' moment that allows the reader to further connect with Wang. It shows he does have a heart, buried under his selfish desires.

Next, is the latter part of the last sentence: "he turned and took the first step toward a magical world."

This is a chapter page turner. What reader wouldn't want to know what the 'magical world' is? This is part of middle strengthening and story building. You want to provide the reader with something at the end of each chapter that will prompt her to go on to the next chapter.

You can see the same technique in the first chapter, last paragraph, last sentence of *Walking Through Walls*: "His thirst for knowledge became a powerful desire to go on an unforgettable journey."

Again, this is a chapter page turner. It provides excitement and curiosity as to what will happen in the following chapters, what's the "unforgettable journey." This hook chapter ending prompts expectation on the reader's part as to what will unfold or happen. This helps keep the reader engaged.

Do you see a pattern of scene building that develops the protagonist and moves the story forward?

CHAPTER FOUR

Chapter four has Wang traveling to the Eternals through an unbelievably thick fog: "Tired and hungry, Wang trudged through fog as thick as porridge."

Okay, let's pause a moment to sidetrack just a bit. I want you to notice that sentence. "Wang trudged through **fog as thick as porridge**." This is a simile.

According to ...*As One Mad With Wine and Other Similes*, by Elyse Sommer and Mike Sommer:

*The simile is, of course, much more than an attention getter. It colors and clarifies ideas by comparing two dissimilar things and does so in a straightforward way by introducing the comparison with the word **like** or **as**—or sometimes with the phrases as **if, as though, is comparable to, can be likened to, akin to, similar to**. This directness makes the simile the most accessible of all figures of speech, a favorite device for both literary and ordinary self-expression.*

While similes are great and an effective writing tool, you don't want to overdo them or use clichés', like 'thin as a reed, 'cute as a button,' 'white as a ghost,' you get the idea. If you can't think of original and effective ones, you shouldn't use similes.

Okay, back on track.

After seven days of traveling through the fog, Wang is out of food:

His stomach growled. This reminded him that he ate the last crust of bread in the morning, or was it yesterday? But thoughts of all the magic he could learn from the Eternal Master soon made his hunger and doubts disappear; they were no match for Wang's wild imagination.

Finally, Wang finds the opening to the mountain path leading to the mountaintop and the Eternals.

Pausing, he looked at the path ahead of him and studied the base of the mountain. Slowly his gaze traveled up and up and up until he could see no further. The mountain loomed above him like a never-ending wall. Its thick giant trees left little space between for a trail.

He stood looking at the obstacle in front of him. A chill ran through his body. Giving a little shake to shed the fear, Wang clutched his fists. *This is what you want; you must follow through.* He pulled his shoulders back, lifted his head, and marched forward. Soon the path behind him was out of sight.

These scenes further emphasize Wang's determination. Although afraid, he marched forward. He might have decided to quit with the obstacles in front of him, but he remained focused on what he wanted. The reader has to give him credit for being determined and not wimping out.

The obstacles are piling up, no food, an almost unsurpassable mountain path, but Wang forges through. He meets the obstacles with determination. Or, you might say 'a stubbornness.'

All these obstacles bring the reader along for the ride, building an emotional connection. They may be wondering at this point if he'll make it to the mountaintop or will something stop him. How will he survive without food?

In the same chapter these questions are answered and he ends up in the presence of the Master Eternal begging for an apprenticeship.

"With all my heart I want to follow you. I can bear anything. I have to be an Eternal. I beg you."

The Master continued staring at Wang. "You seem determined to become my student. I accept you for an apprenticeship. But you must remember, the training is long and hard, and without much reward."

This is the end of the chapter and sets the scene for Chapter Five – what's involved in being an Eternal apprentice. The reader may be thinking that Wang doesn't like work, he's lazy. And, he wants to be rich. This apprenticeship has little reward.

Again, this creates engagement and is moving the plot forward. Another obstacle in Wang's path to riches . . . work.

Can you see, just through these little quotes, how the story is moving forward, how the middle is strengthening, how Wang is overcoming obstacles to reach his goal? This is story building and keeps the connection with the reader going.

CHAPTER FIVE

This is where Wang and the reader get a glimpse of magic. Don't forget that the reader is along for the ride and finds out things as Wang does.

Wang is brought to his room by one of the Master's attendants and Wang questions him:

"The temple does not look too large from outside. How is it that it is so grand inside?"

"Not all things are as they appear," answered the boy.

Chapter Five also goes into some detail of the work that Wang and the other apprentices must do each day, and shows a couple of other tiny bits of magic, but as of yet, the apprentices themselves have not been taught any.

This has Wang up-in-arms and after a couple of days he decides to leave and prompts the next chapter, demonstrating his impatience.

CHAPTER SIX

Chen jumped off his cot and grabbed Wang's arm. "Wang, you are being too hasty. You must give it more time. Remember, the rewards will be much greater than the sacrifice. You cannot give up. A man must finish what he commits to. At least wait until morning."

This shows another element of Chen's character – he's sensible, honorable, and patient.

These characteristics are also brought up a bit earlier in the story and the differences in Wang and Chen allow for good chemistry. Having characters with varying personalities is a good way to keep your story realistic.

It also allows for engaging conversations and 'back and forths.' If Chen were similar to Wang, what engagement would there be. And, who would prompt Wang onto the 'right' path? As I mentioned earlier, the actions and reactions of the characters help build their individual characters and that of the characters they interact with.

In this chapter Chen cannot convince Wang to stay, but when he goes to find the Master to tell him he's leaving, he accidently sees the kind of magic he's been longing for. This motivates him to stay.

Then in one swift motion, his hands landed on top of his head. "This is it. This is the magic I need. I cannot go now. I must learn to walk through walls."

Notice the 'hands' characteristic again. It's important, when creating certain quirks for characters, to be consistent with them.

And, this is another conflict or motivating factor that leads Wang onto his character's path, this time to stay as an apprentice. Now, all he wants to do is see more magic, and learn it.

This is all strengthening the middle through ongoing inner conflict. He wants to go, he wants to stay. He wants to learn magic, but he hasn't. It all steadily moves Wang's character and the story further along.

The chapter progresses with Wang doing his daily work, day in and day out.

Days turned into weeks, and weeks turned into months. Wang wished to see the Master perform more magic, but that did not happen either. With the passing months Wang grew impatient, discouraged, and even angry.

This is the end of Chapter Six. It should have the reader feeling disappointed along with Wang and wondering what he'll do. This will motivate the reader to move on to the next chapter.

Each scene, each chapter should move the story forward, while keeping the reader engaged. And, if you noticed Wang did get glimpses of magic, which helps keep the reader satisfied.

CHAPTER SEVEN

This is where the reader finally sees Wang get what he's wanted all along, to learn magic.

It's a year since he became an apprentice and Wang is fed-up. He again decides to leave and tells the Master. But he asks, as compensation for all his hard work, to be taught one magic feat . . . walking through walls.

The Master agrees and this chapter shows Wang learning to walk through walls. There is one caveat though: he can only use the magic to help others, not for evil.

Wang stared at the wall and repeated the formula. He took several steps toward the wall. He closed his eyes and quickened his step. In a matter of seconds he felt a thickness all around him, like walking through water or sand. Then it vanished. He opened his eyes.

"I did it. I did it! I DID IT." Excitement boiled in Wang like lava in a volcano.

The reader should at this point be happy for Wang and feel his excitement. And, it should provide satisfaction in that they finally see him learn the magic that has been hinted at all along.

So, Wang's a very happy camper and leaves the temple to go home. His intent is to use that magic to become RICH!

At this part of the story it's heading toward the very peak of the story arc. Wang got what he wanted, but the question is, will he use it to take from others to become rich.

So, there you have the building and strengthening of a story's middle.

It's important to be aware that some stories are much more action packed and it will be the action furthering the story along, whether caused by the antagonist or the protagonist.

In addition the protagonist's reactions to obstacles thrown in his way will also steadily move the story forward and strengthen its middle. More and more bits of information will be included letting the reader 'in on it.'

Conflict can be external and internal. Using the character of Chen again, if he were the protagonist in *Walking Through Walls*, his conflict would be external – the neighboring warriors. This would cause external responses and actions on Chen's part.

Note though that **conflict doesn't have to be in the form of a person.** A protagonist may be fighting against a natural disaster or struggling to rebuild after a natural disaster. Maybe he's coping with the loss of a family member or pet, or an illness.

Brooks explains that "conflict is the essence of effective fiction" (*Story Engineering*, 150). Defining this conflict and striving to overcome it is the primary mission of your middle, levels two and three of your story's structure.

Upping the Stakes Ups the Tension, the Antagonist, and Subplots

RISING TENSION

IT'S THE ONGOING conflicts or complications and the protagonist's efforts to overcome each one that works toward building and strengthening your middle.

The genre you're writing in will determine the depth and complexity of the complications.

Each complication should bring a little more risk, upping the stakes. The protagonist should have to put forth more effort and have more to lose with each additional complication – this creates tension. It will take a combination of wins and losses to keep the reader satisfied. If 80 percent of your story is the protagonist repeatedly losing and being pushed further and further back, you may lose reader interest. So, have him win one or two battles.

An example of this is when Wang decided to first leave his apprenticeship. Accidently seeing the Master perform magic motivated him to stay – this was a little win. This little win makes the next complication or struggle more significant – the protagonist is a bit more invested in overcoming it, which will have the reader more invested in the story.

And, going back to <u>Margot Finke's</u> article "What to Aim For When Writing," it's the slow build-up of tension that gives good pace. "Dropping hints and clues builds tension, which in turn moves your story along. Short, punchy sentences give better pace than longwinded lines."

Remember that an important job of the story's middle is to show how the protagonist grows and changes. Challenging your characters in ways they don't expect will force them to grow.

Note: Picture books are so short, it's okay to have the protagonist lose all the battles until the final one which he overcomes as in *Stephanie's Ponytail*.

THE ANTAGONIST

Within parts two and three, your antagonist will also become developed. This is another factor of building and strengthening your middle.

According to <u>Laura Backes</u>, in her article "Crafting a Worthy Foe," an antagonist is "any force working against your main character, pulling her away from her goal. And while your plot should have lots of obstacles that pop up, throwing roadblocks in your protagonist's way, the antagonist is another fully-developed character with an agenda of his own."

The antagonist's sole purpose cannot simply be to block the protagonist's attempts at reaching his goal. The antagonist needs to have layers just like the protagonist and other secondary characters. This means he'll have both good and bad qualities. Maybe within the story, the 'bad' qualities sharply overshadow the good.

Your secondary characters need to have their own motives for being in the story, for their actions and reactions.

Think of a real life situation, say an office. The protagonist, Bob, wants the new 'higher' position that just opened up. But, so does the antagonist, Jim. He undermines and sabotages Bob in whatever ways he can.

But, why does Jim want the position so badly that he resorts to nasty tactics? What's his underlying motive for undermining Bob? Is it purely because he wants the higher pay and prestige that goes along with the new position? Or, is part of it that he dislikes Bob? Or, is it a combination? Does he owe money to a loan shark and desperately needs money? Does he have a child with a disease and needs money to help him?

Answering these character questions and the other questions in your 'character interview' will help fully develop your antagonist. And, through the revelation of his character, it may possibly reveal additional information about the protagonist.

Keep in mind though that for young children, the picture book group, plot and characters should be simplistic and easy to recognize.

An example of a simple external situation is Margot Finke's book *Ruthie and the Hippo's Fat Behind*. It's about a little girl who just moved with her family. She had to leave all her friends, her school, everything she was familiar and comfortable with. This is an external situation that causes internal conflict and external reactions.

SUBPLOTS

There may also be subplots in genres for middle grade and young adult. Chen's problem if developed more would be a subplot. For the younger age group simple is always better.

According to Wikipedia, "A subplot is a secondary plot strand that is a supporting side story for any story or main plot. Subplots may connect to main plots, in either time and place or in thematic significance. Subplots often involve supporting characters, those besides the protagonist or antagonist."

Subplots take up less of the action and are of minor significance, which makes them distinguishable from the main plot. And, as mentioned, the stories for younger children do not have subplots. Short stories usually don't have subplots either.

Subplots can be used to add more depth, adding another layer to the main plot. They can also be used to explore characters and their relationships. Also, while your main plot must be neatly tied-up at the end, subplots don't need the same end-all resolution. Although it's never a good idea to have the reader wondering about 'so and so' at the end of the story.

My personal take on writing is to tie-up every loose end whether part of the main plot or a subplot.

Balance in Writing: The Major Elements

THERE ARE FIVE major elements to a story and it's the combination of these elements that make the story complete, interesting, and considered good writing. Too much of one or not enough of another can affect the readers ability to connect with the story.

So, what are the major elements of a story?

THE MAJOR ELEMENTS OF A STORY

1. Protagonist
2. Setting
3. Plot
4. Point of view
5. Theme

The Protagonist: This is the main character. He needs to be introduced at the very beginning of the story when writing for picture books through simpler middle grade. Using your imagination you can make him unique. He can have particular mannerisms or quirks, or even distinct physical attributes. You can also make him likeable or unsavory, but remember you will need the reader to be able to create a connection to him. It's this connection that will prompt the reader to continue reading on. Your protagonist needs to be real...believable.

The Setting: This will establish the time and place the story takes place. The setting can create a feeling and mood – if you're writing about swashbuckling pirates, your reader will be in a certain mind set. The same holds true for any other setting you choose. It will be intrinsic to the plot/conflict and will help establish vivid imagery for the reader.

The Plot: This is the meat of the story – the forward movement, the conflict or struggle that drives the protagonist toward his goal. This involves any danger, suspense, romance, or other reader grabbing occurrence. The conflict can be emotional (an internal struggle – a tormented soul) or physical (from an external/outside force – good against evil).

Point of View: This establishes the point of view or perspective from which the story is being told. It's important to make this clear. Even if you 'kind of' have two main characters, there needs to be one who is primary in order to keep clarity within the story. And, it will be from the protagonist or primary character's point of view that the story will be told.

The Theme: This establishes what is important to the story. It usually evolves along with the story and the protagonist's progression. If Jesus is your protagonist, establishing and promoting Christianity might be the theme. It might be the story's view on life and the people/characters the protagonist encounters. It is the idea the author wants the reader to take away with him/her.

Utilizing each of these elements can create a unique, fascinating, and memorable story. Just like the ingredients in a cooking recipe, writing has its own set of ingredients that produce a wonderful end product. A pinch here, a dab there – you hold the unique recipe to your story.

What Makes a Good Fiction Story:
Plot Driven or Character Drive?

STORIES CAN BE plot driven or character driven, so which is the best formula to use when writing a story? Knowing a little about both methods should help in making a decision.

Plot Driven Story

A story's plot moves the story forward, from point A to point B. It doesn't necessarily have to be in a straight line. In fact, a course that twists and turns is much better. This type of plot creates movement and interest. It's the twists and turns that will keep the forward momentum fresh, as well as create anticipation. Anticipation will hold a reader's attention.

The plot also provides reasons and explanations for the occurrences in the story, as well as offers conflict and obstacles that the protagonist must overcome to hopefully create growth. These elements create a connection with the reader. It entices the reader to keep turning the pages.

Without a plot it is difficult to create growth and movement for the protagonist. It might be comparable to looking at a still photo. The photo may be beautiful and may even conjure up emotions in the viewer, but how long do you think it would hold a reader's attention?

Along with this, the plot molds the protagonist. It causes growth and movement in the character. Assume you have a timid woman who through circumstances the plot transforms into a brave, strong, forceful hero. Where would the story be without the events that lead this timid woman to move past herself and into a new existence?

Character Driven Story

On the other hand, a character driven story creates a bond between the protagonist and reader. It is the development and growth of the character, the character's personal journey, which motivates the reader to connect. There doesn't need to be twists and turns, or fireworks. The reader becomes involved with the character and this is all the enticement the reader needs to keep reading.

In addition to this, the character works hand-in-hand with the plot to move the story forward. As the character begins her transformation the plot moves in the same direction.

In some instances, such as short stories, a character driven story can work amazingly well. *The Story of an Hour* by Kate Chopin is an example of this. In cases such as this, the connection developed between the character and the reader can be more than enough to satisfy the reader. But, all in all, it seems to be the combined efforts of a well plotted and character driven story that works the best.

The Best of Both Worlds

According to science fiction and fantasy writer, <u>L.E. Modesitt, Jr.</u>, "The best fiction should be an intertwined blend of character, plot, setting, and style."

I agree. All elements of a story working together create stories that will be remembered.

All the aspects of a story should complement each other, should move each other forward to a satisfying conclusion, and should draw the reader in.

As mentioned earlier, if you have an action packed plot driven story, but it lacks believable and sympathetic characters, you're story will be lacking. The same holds true if you have a believable and sympathetic character, but the story lacks movement, it will usually also fall short. As with all things in life balance is necessary, the same holds true when writing a story.

Theme and Your Story

THEME CAN BE a frightening topic. Do you have a theme in mind before striking the first key? Or, do you write your first draft and then decide what the theme is? Do you have a problem deciding what the theme is, even after you're in revisions?

In an article, "What We Talk About When We Talk About Theme," in the *Writer's Chronicle*, May 2010, Eileen Pollack discusses theme:

"The concrete elements of any story constitute its plot—Character A, in Village B, is torn by a specific conflict that gives rise to a series of concrete actions through which she relieves that stress. The more general question raised in the reader's mind by this specific character acting out this specific plot constitutes the story's *aboutness*—or, dare I say, it's theme."

This description of the elements of a story holds true for any fiction work, including children's stories. The elements, woven together with theme as the foundation, is what makes the reader continue on, turning the pages . . . it's what makes the reader care.

According to Pollack, "Theme is the writer's answer to the reader's rude, *So what?*"

And, if the theme is poignant and captures what some or many people actually do, this will allow the reader to recognize the situation and actions and she will be engaged. Hopefully, the readers will be able to take the theme, however subtle it is, away with them.

For those worried about the theme affecting the story's natural flow, Pollack advises deciding on your theme after your first draft. Once you have your theme in hand, go over your story again and again. You can now let the theme subtly permeate your story. Pollack goes on to say, "The most powerful use of theme is the way it allows you to fill in your characters' inner lives."

Literary agent Mary Kole, in her blog at Kidlit.com, also sheds light on the worrisome theme:

"When you revise, think about what your work is saying. You've got to have a reason for writing it. There should be distinct themes and ideas that you could point to as the center of your book. [...] Once you know what these are — and you usually won't until you've started revising — you can use them as a lens. [...] A theme for your work should color everything in it, subtly, especially the descriptions."

So, making it as simple as possible, theme is the story's purpose, it's the story's overall main topic. And, each reader may see something different in your story.

Below are some common themes:

- Right vs. wrong
- Crime doesn't pay
- Loss (death, divorce, etc.)
- Moving (home, job, etc.)
- Man vs. nature (Survival)
- Man vs. man (Survival)
- Man vs. technology

- Man vs. Environment (Survival)
- Love, friendship, family
- We can be our own worst enemy
- Selfishness vs. altruism
- The 'wanting more' syndrome and its consequence (Greed)
- Coming of Age
- Religion
- Moral lesson

So, there you have, after you've written your story and are working on revisions, if you haven't gotten it yet, your theme should become evident.

Section Four Resources

HERE ARE RELEVANT links to several helpful articles:

The Three Layers of Story Engineering, Architecture, and Art
http://storyfix.com/the-three-layers-of-story-engineering-architecture-and-art

The Basics of Plot: A Classical Approach
http://educationwantstobefree.blogspot.com/2011/09/basics-of-plot-classical-approach.html

Bad Obstacles
http://kidlit.com/2012/02/27/bad-obstacles/

Are You Giving Readers the Tools to Understand Your Story?
http://www.helpingwritersbecomeauthors.com/are-you-giving-readers-tools-to/

Shore-up Your Sagging Middle
http://www.writersonthemove.com/2011/08/shore-up-your-sagging-middle.html

Theme, Imagery and Description
http://kidlit.com/2009/12/21/theme-imagery-and-description/

Writing on a Theme
http://kidlit.com/2011/11/07/writing-on-a-theme/

Vary Your Sentences: Start with a Different Part of Speech
http://4rvreading-writingnewsletter.blogspot.com/2011/11/vary-your-sentences-start-with.html

Put action in books for children and teens
http://4rvreading-writingnewsletter.blogspot.com/2011/08/put-action-in-books-for-children-and.html

3 Ways to Know When to End Your Chapters
http://writersdigest.com/article/3-ways-to-know-when-to-end-your-chapters/

A Balance of Action and Information
http://kidlit.com/2011/09/28/a-balance-of-action-and-information/

Backstory in Description, Dialogue, and Flashback
http://joanyedwards.wordpress.com/2011/10/19/backstory-in-description-dialogue-and-flashback/

Section Four Assignment

— — — — — — — — — — — —

1. USING THE work you started on the assignments for Sections One through Three, develop the story further, to around 750 to 1000 words (three to four pages). It will have your beginning, your characters, and conflict – it will have all the elements needed for an engaging story.

It will include Levels One, Two, and Three of a story's structure: setup, response, and attack.

After you do this assignment, read it and check for relevancy and clarity.

- Is every scene needed?
- Does each scene move the story forward?
- Are your characters developed?
- Do your characters help move the story forward?
- Is it understandable?
- Are your characters and the story engaging?

If possible have a family member or friend read it to get a fresh viewpoint.

* You'll be adding the Resolution/Ending to this story as your assignment for Section Five.

======

2. If you haven't yet (and you should have), join a children's critique group.

Do an online search. If you're a member of the Society of Children's Book Writers and Illustrators (SCBWI), they have a great forum where you can find critique groups.

Take note though, you will be required to critique other members' work in addition to having your own work critiqued. And, each group has their own way of doing things.

Section Five

YOU REACHED YOUR *story's climax, now you're bringing it home: The resolution.*

This is the part of the story where the hero triumphs. And you need to make sure you create a satisfying ending. Leaving a reader with a 'huh?' feeling risks the chance of them never picking up another book by you again.

Section Five Content:

Introduction
Finding the Ending
Examining Endings
Recommended Reading
Being a Writer: Learn the Craft of Writing
Writing Goals, Detours, and Opportunity Costs
Writing for Children: 10 Basic Rules
Your Assignment

Introduction to Section Five

You've had quite a journey to this point and you're at the peak of your story arc. This is the beginning of your ending.

Now what?

Well, now comes your resolution, your conclusion. And, there are a few things you need to do to make sure your reader goes away satisfied.

The resolution is where your protagonist finally 'gets it.' He figures out how to overcome the final obstacle, or he acquirers the knowledge, tools, and/or help he needs to triumph.

Along with this, the ending needs to tie-up all the loose ends, any foreshadowing or hints of things that may have been mentioned. You don't want your reader to be scratching her head and leave with an unsatisfied feeling. That's just bad for your writing career!

The loose ends that need to be tied-up will include any subplots you have going on. Not that they need to be completely resolved like your protagonist's conflicts, but they at least need to be addressed.

In *Walking Through Walls*, Chen needed to save his village and his sister, and he wanted Wang's help. Wang declined – his own selfish motives were more important. While this does kind of tie-up this subplot, it leaves a vacant space for readers: what happens to Chen's sister? Will Wang change his mind?

The latter question is answered in the ending, but the one about Chen's sister remains open. While this doesn't quite tie everything up in a nice little package, it does leave the opportunity for a sequel to the story.

This can be a double-edged sword. On the one hand it's advantageous to leave room for growth, a sequel, but on the other hand you don't want to leave the reader hanging. To help avoid this, it's a good idea to make the briefest mention of a particular subplot, if it won't be satisfactorily resolved at the end of the story. And, only use it if it's absolutely needed.

In *Walking Through Walls*, the tiny mention of Chen's dilemma is required. It sets up Chen's character – his motive for being an Eternal apprentice.

Okay, I got sidetracked again, but it's important information that needed to be mentioned. Back on track now.

Section Five deals with the fourth level or part of the story structure discussed earlier This is where your protagonist becomes the hero. Your story has gone through the first three parts of the story structure and your protagonist has:

- Identified the conflict/obstacle blocking the path to his goal.
- Responded to the conflict by devising a plan: either striving to overcome it or running/hiding from it. He's the Wanderer or Victim. He's on the defense.
- Had enough. He's learned what he needed to or he's acquired the means necessary to take action. He now becomes the Attacker. He confronts his obstacles head on – he goes into battle-mode.
- Now, in the Resolution, he becomes the Hero. He triumphs.

At this point, the protagonist has grown and developed the courage, skills, knowledge or other heroic tools needed to have the solution to the problem and be victorious. He's got the last puzzle piece.

It's important to remember that in children's writing, as mentioned a couple of times already, the protagonist must be the one who figures it out, who overcomes, who reaches the goal, who triumphs – you get the idea.

For the younger genres, the picture book, the last page should have an obvious ending, meaning it needs to "come to a natural, logical conclusion. The action should end at a definitive moment, with no plot points left hanging," according to <u>Laura Backes</u>, in her article, "Writing Powerful Endings."

Important note: While this is the part of the story that puts it all together, you can't use the ending to 'tell' the reader the actual lessons the protagonist learned, or how he actually grew. The reader will 'get' this message from your well-structured story, from watching the protagonist's growing or the transformation process. If your protagonist's name is Tony, your last sentence can't say, "Tony learned his lesson; he'll now go to school every day and apply himself."

You need to give the reader credit for being intelligent. You don't have to hit her over the head. In fact, this will only alienate your reader. And, don't let your story or ending be preachy.

Let your ending be your ending – don't add explanations.

Finding the Ending

THE STORY ARC'S peak is the beginning of the ending. It's the scene in which your protagonist, through action, chooses his final path to victory. It's the turning point that pushes him to become the hero.

In addition, it should have the highest peak of action, whether physical or emotional, or both. And, it should have your reader sitting on the edge of her seat. This doesn't necessarily mean literally, it means the reader's emotions and engagement should be peaked and in full throttle.

If you've been working from an outline, you will know in what direction your ending is heading. You'll know the outcome and will be filling in the blanks.

Another way to find your ending is if you know the theme of your story. If you didn't start your story with a theme in mind, maybe by this point it's become evident and will guide you to a logical conclusion.

In regard to a story's theme, editor Cheryl B. Klein, in her book *Second Sight*, explains that there are two related categories to the theme of a story or the take-away value. There's the "message or moral," and there's the "emotional" (95).

Walking Through Walls has a 'message'. The *Captain Underpants* series, as Klein points out, is for pure fun and laughter – it's theme is 'emotional' (95).

For a satisfying ending, think of the natural, forward-moving progression of occurrences that will follow part three of your story. Imagine what you want the ending to look like.

Often, your ending will write itself from what transpired before. As mentioned above, if you created an outline, there's no real imagery necessary on your part – the outline is the roadmap to your ending.

A helpful way to see how 'good endings' are structured is to analyze endings from traditionally and newly published children's books, along with the classics. Effective endings are thought provoking.

Endings may also link back to the beginning of the story through idea or word repetition, strengthening the story, as in *Stephanie's Ponytail*. And endings definitely tie-up all loose ends and will usually tie-up, for the most part, all subplots.

Here's a checklist you can go through to help get a sense of what your ending should reflect and how to get there:

1. Reread your story and make sure you have a character sheet with full details for each main and secondary character. Take special note of any situations and subplots you created for each character, among the characters, or between your characters. Included should be the motives and stakes for each significant character.

2. Tie-up all loose ends for the main character/s. Unless the story itself has taken you through to a satisfying ending, you'll need to decide how you want your main characters to end up. Will the ending be a no-thought-process on the readers' part, where you leave no room for projection? Or, will it be a satisfying, yet left up to the reader's interpretation ending? Whichever you choose, all conflicts and situations must be resolved in a satisfying fashion.

If you're going with a 'message' ending, avoid making it preachy. Make your message subtle - readers don't like to be preached to.

3. Tie-up all loose ends for secondary characters. While I did mention it's not essential to conclude minor characters' situations completely, it does help if you at least tie it in a bow, if not a knot.

Readers will feel more satisfied it they know whether the fight between secondary characters Joe and Tom was resolved. Or, suppose a secondary character lost her dog early on in the story, you should let the reader know what happened with that situation. This leaves an overall feeling of everything being tied-up. It provides closure.

Subplots should be tied-up before or at the same time as the primary plot concludes.

4. If you're unsure of how to resolve an open situation: if it's an external situation between characters, confrontation is a good way to help the characters work it out for themselves. As you're having the characters react to one another the resolution should present itself.

If you're stuck, ask the help of your critique partners. A fresh perspective can do wonders.

5. Pay special attention to what was promised to the reader – all promises need to be fulfilled. Along with this keep track of all hints and foreshadows.

As an example: in *Walking Through Walls*, along with the promise of magic, there was the issue of Wang's character faults that needed to be addressed.

In addition, there were a number of hints of 'more to come' that are very subtle. It would have been easy for me to miss fulfilling one of them if I wasn't very careful.

6. Don't introduce any new characters or conflict in the ending.

7. If writing for the younger child, it's essential that you provide a clear-cut happy ending. This is a must.

If it's for the latter MG or YA age group, it doesn't have to be a 'pure sunshine' ending, it can be a 'partly sunny' ending. What this means is if you're writing a romance, the main characters don't have to end up together for it to be a happy ending. It will all depend on how you write it. Maybe they both – equally – decide they don't work together romantically, but still remain best of friends. If your main characters are satisfied, your reader will be satisfied. Although, it's important to mention that most readers do want a 'sunshine' ending.

In the article "Endings" at Eclectics.com, New York Times bestselling author Lori Handeland spoke about the importance of delivering on what was promised in the story.

In regard to romance novels Handeland urges writers to make the endings 'sunshine' all the way. "I've judged several times in the Golden Heart competition and I've actually had to write on manuscripts 'Don't kill off the hero at the end of the book.' It makes editors cranky, not to mention a reader who's been promised the happy ending inherent in the words 'romance novel.'"

There are some YA books with realistic endings that are 'cloudy' or even 'stormy,' but as Handeland advises, most editors and readers want the 'happy ending.'

8. While going through the ending process, if it doesn't write itself or dictate what type of ending it needs, you'll have to come up with one.

Do you want a quiet, yet effective ending? Do you want an all-around happy ending? Do you want a more realistic ending? Think about how you want it to end.

And, keep in mind that not all endings will read or feel the same. As the saying goes, 'different strokes for different folks,' so it goes with endings. Some will be a slow simmer to a satisfying ending, some will be a blow torch or fireworks approach, and others will lie somewhere in between.

You'll need to pay attention to the story and the logical, fluid ending it's calling for.

Whichever you choose, just remember it needs to tie-up all loose ends, leave all your characters satisfied, and leave your reader satisfied.

9. Readers don't like to be left hanging, and they want and expect a logical conclusion to the story. Be sure to go through each step carefully. And in the ending process, write it through 'showing' rather than 'telling.' Make it a fluid part of the story.

10. Your protagonist should have transformed or grown significantly from his journey to victory. Check to make sure this is evident in your ending.

11. If you're not happy with the ending you've written, analyze it to see why, then either fix what's wrong or rewrite it until you feel it's' got it all. Take advantage of your critique group if needed.

Examining Endings

WHILE THERE ARE many excellent examples of great endings, I've chosen a few I like.

SLEEPLESS IN SEATTLE

Sleepless in Seattle is a 1993 movie based on a story by Jeff Arch. With inspiration from the 1957 *An Affair to Remember*, this romantic comedy is an excellent example of the parts of the story structure and a highly climactic ending.

Part One: The opening has Annie, the protagonist, and her fiancé visiting family for the holidays. They drive separately to the finance's family and as Annie's driving, she hears Sam, the other main character talking about his deceased wife. This defines her conflict – it's the inciting incident. She develops a connection to Sam and subconsciously questions her own engagement.

Part Two: Annie is troubled by the conflict and finds out all she can about Sam. She even travels to meet him, but chicken's out. She struggles with her relationship and finally breaks off her engagement. She is in the 'figuring out' stage. She's reacting to the conflict.

Part Three: Annie is in 'attack mode.' She builds up her courage and flies to Seattle to meet Sam. But, it doesn't happen that simply. By the ending, the viewer is vested in the outcome. They are rooting for Annie to finally meet Sam. They want the happy ending.

But, when Annie gets to the Empire State Building, it's closed. She does get to go to the observation deck, but Sam and his son aren't there. She's crushed . . . and so is the audience; they're screaming, "He just left. Run after him!"

Do you see the build-up? The story tension is peaked – emotions are soaring. This is the beginning of the end.

Part Four: Then, the elevator door opens and it's Sam. He takes her hand in his, and ... it's magic. They enter the elevator looking into each other's eyes. Everyone is ecstatic. That's a great climax and delivery, and it plays out at the very end of the story. It's a 'fireworks' ending.

This is an example to follow: go for brevity in your ending. Once the climatic incident and its satisfying delivery occurs, wind it up quickly. If you try to stretch it out, it will only take away from the climax and diminish the reader's emotions.

This is not to say all stories should end quickly, some stories don't lend themselves to this type of ending. *Walking Through Walls* is one that doesn't.

The following is an analysis of the ending of *Walking Through Walls*.

WALKING THROUGH WALLS

Walking Through Walls has a slow-building ending. We'll look at the last three chapters.

Chapter Eight

Still in part three of the story, armed with the tool he'll need to get rich, he leaves his Eternal apprenticeship to embark on his road to power and wealth.

During his journey home, Wang devises a plan to steal from the rich.

Chapter Nine

Wang is resolved to go through with his plan:

It will be easy to take valuables by walking through walls. First I will make sure no one is home. Then I will walk right in. Locked doors will not stop me. No one can stop me.

So much for Master Eternal's warning that the magic can only be used for 'good.'

Now at home he puts his plan into action. He studies his 'victim' and his victim's movements. This is still level three of the story structure. He's in the attack level.

The day finally arrives and Wang waits in hiding until the merchant leaves his home.

Gazing intently at the cottage, he waited until the merchant left for work. *Now is my chance. This is what I have wanted since I was a young boy.* But Wang's feet stayed firmly planted, not moving an inch.

This is the peak of the story arc and the beginning of the end. This is Wang's definitive moment. Will he steal from the merchant? Will his conscience rule? This is the fork in the road between ruin and victory. And, as mentioned early it doesn't need to involve 'fireworks.'

He shook his body as if trying to get rid of an outer skin. He repeated the magic formula and walked toward the wall. Suddenly, he stopped. His thoughts turned to the master and Chen. *The master gave the purple-tipped axe to those whose hearts were not YET pure. And, Chen needs my help to rescue Yin.*

There you have it, Wang's first step onto the hero's road.

Chapter Ten

Confused and very troubled, Wang seeks the village elder's guidance. He reveals all that's gone on and his evil intentions. The elder has been waiting for him and helps Wang to see all he's missed and where his true fate lies.

This is a slow and very revealing concluding chapter. Every loose end, even the subtlest of hints, hints that many readers may not have picked up on, is brought to light and explained. The ending delivers in spades.

Now, let's take a quick look at the powerful ending of Thelma and Louise.

THELMA AND LOUISE

Thelma and Louise doesn't necessarily follow the classic four part structure of a story, as parts two and three are both comprised of the protagonists reacting to the conflict – running from the police - it does however have a powerful ending.

As with *Sleepless in Seattle*, the climax is at the very end of the story. The turning point has the protagonists at the end of the road, literally. They have a choice of surrendering to the police or driving over a cliff. The ending stunned many a movie goer and created a story that wasn't easily forgotten.

While this type of ending isn't appropriate for a children's book, it does show the structure of a short and effective ending. Parts One, Two, and Three of the story structure made up around 90 - 95 percent of the story, possibly more. Then at the very end, the conclusion was revealed. The protagonists chose their path, their destiny.

As mentioned earlier, your story and ending are only limited by your imagination. And, if you use award-winning books or movies as a model for your story, it can help raise the cap on your own imagination.

Now we'll look at a couple of Picture Books.

STEPHANIE'S PONYTAIL

In Section Four we discussed how *Stephanie's Ponytail* went through the first three parts of the story structure. Each time she resolved to be unique, she was met with opposition. And for each obstacle, she came up with a solution only to be blocked again.

This is also a great example of having the protagonist lose some of the battles. This strategy makes each subsequent battle or conflict have higher stakes, higher emotions.

The conclusion of this wonderful picture book has Stephanie using her 'smarts' to outsmart her classmates. And, as mentioned earlier, in most picture books the ending plays out on the very last page.

Stephanie threatened she would cut off all her hair, shave her head. And, as follows in all predictable books, her classmates do what they have done throughout the story, they copy what Stephanie says she will do. This time they shave their heads. But Stephanie comes to school the next day with a "ponytail coming right out the back."

The takeaway value might be that with perseverance you can overcome your obstacles. The conclusion to *Stephanie's Ponytail* is funny and clever. The takeaway value might also be 'emotion,' as the ending illustration has the class angry and chasing her. It's sure to make the young reader laugh. Some stories are for pure entertainment.

CAPS FOR SALE

Caps for Sales is another predictable picture book. A hat peddler sits under a tree to take a nap. He naps with all the caps on his head. When he awakes his caps are gone, except for his own cap on his head. Sitting in the branches of the tree above him there are a group of monkeys. Each of them is wearing one of his caps.

The peddler shook his finger at the monkeys and yelled to give back his caps. The monkeys shook their fingers back at him and made noises.

Next the peddler shook both hands at the monkeys. The monkeys shook their hands at the peddler.

This went on for a few more actions on the peddler's part. And, for each action the peddler took, the monkeys mimicked him.

The peddler got so infuriated he took the cap that sat on his head and through it to the ground. Each monkey mimicked the peddler and threw their hats to the ground. The peddler picked up all the hats, put them back on his head and walked away, off to sell his caps.

This is another example of the protagonist losing the battles until he finally wins in the end. It's also an excellent example of predictability, which younger kids love. They love to be able to guess, based on what has been happening, what's going to happen next.

Examine and Model the Classics

Again, examine the classics, award-winning books, and newly traditionally published books. See how their story moves into a logical and satisfying ending. There are authors who use books like *The Three Little Pigs* and *Goldilock and the Three Bears* as a model for writing their own stories.

Looking at these two stories in particular, you can clearly see the 'rule of three.' This is a common formula for children's writing. Elements of the story are set up in 'threes.'

The protagonist finds himself in three situations or conflicts and it's the third one that he's able to overcome.

Find what works for you.

There you have it. We've gone through all four parts of a story's structure and it should guide you on your own children's fiction writing journey.

Do your best by learning the craft of writing and applying that knowledge to your writing. Follow the 'proven' strategies for creating a well-structured and engaging story and write, write, write.

"While all books must fulfill the qualities we laid out earlier, with interesting characters and story, good writing, and a point to its telling (whether emotional or moral) . . . not every book has to be deep. Not every book has to be funny. Not every book has to make you cry. Not every book has to be Harry Potter" (*Second Sight*, 95).

Whether your aim is to take the traditionally published route or self-publish, creating a quality story is a must.

I've included a reading list you might look into, along with a couple of bonus articles.

Children's Fiction: Recommended Reading List

PICTURE BOOKS:

Stephanie's Ponytail by Robert Munsch
Owen by Kevin Henkes (received a Caldecott award)
Strega Nona by Tomie dePaola (received a Caldecott award)
More Parts by Tedd Arnold
David Goes to School by David Shannon
Frederico, the Mouse Violinist by Mayra Calvani
Ruthie and the Hippo's Fat Behind by Margot Finke
The Kissing Hand by Audrey Penn (New York Times #1 Bestseller)
Five Little Monkeys Jumping on the Bed by Eileen Christelow
Day's End Lullaby by Karen Cioffi
The Pea in the Peanut Butter by Allyn Stotz
The Runaway Bunny by Margaret Wise Brown
Where the Wild Things Are by Maurice Sendak
Fancy Nancy by Jane O'Connor
Caps for Sale by Esphyr Slobodkina

EARLY READERS

Clarice Bean, that's me by Lauren Child
The Boxcar Children by Gertrude Chandler Warne
The Stink Series by Megan McDonald
The Berenstain Bears series by Stan and Jan Berenstain
The Dr. Seuss series by Dr. Seuss

CHAPTER BOOKS AND MIDDLE GRADE

Walking Through Walls by Karen Cioffi (Children's Literary Classics Silver Award)
A Single Shard by Linda Sue Park (awarded the Newbery Medal)
Winn-Dixie by Kate DiCamillo (Received a Newbery Honor)
Frindle by Andrew Clements
How to Eat Fried Worms by Thomas Rockwell
The Chocolate Touch by Patrick Skene Catling
The Whipping Boy by Sid Fleischman (awarded the Newbery Medal)
The Lucky Baseball: My Story in a Japanese-American Internment Camp by Suzanne Lieurance
The Stonekeeper (Amulet, Book 1) by Kazu Kibuishi
Diary of a Wimpy Kid series by Jeff Kinney
Alvin Ho by Lenore Look
The Judy Blume series

YOUNG ADULT BOOKS

An Audience for Einstein by Mark Wakely
The Rock of Realm by Lea Schizas
The Power of Six by Pittacus Lore
The Kane Chronicles by Rick Riordan
The *Twilight* series by Stephenie Meyer
The latter books in the *Harry Potter* series

The books listed within each category are in no particular order and there are many, many, many other great examples you can read. You can also visit your local library and ask the librarian for popular children's and young adult books. Pay special attention to award-winning books and recently published books.

Reading children's books will provide insight into what works and what type of books publishers are looking for, in regard to recently published books. Be aware that what worked 10 years ago may not be what today's publishers are looking for today. But, award-winning books and the classics are always good models.

Learning any craft takes time and practice, writing is a craft that needs to be learned. Take the time to do it right. Take the time to learn the craft of writing.

On the following pages, I've included information that hasn't been covered yet and that will help you on your children's writing journey. There may also be some content that has already been mention - repetition is a key to learning.

Being a Writer: Learn the Craft of Writing

In the June 2010 issue of *The Writer*, author Jane Yolen discussed the need to learn the craft of writing in an article titled, "Dedicate Yourself to a Writing Apprenticeship." She explained that the process is slow and long, but is necessary to being a writer, to learning the craft of writing.

If you're wondering what **the craft of writing is**, it's proper writing technique, grammar, and style. These writing elements include structure, formatting, clarity, and in fiction writing, plot, character development, point of view, and dialogue. Even knowing the particulars in the genre you write is important.

So, what exactly is the meaning of the word 'craft?'

Wikipedia's definition is, "A **craft** is a branch of a profession that requires some particular kind of skilled work."

Merriam-Webster refers to 'craft' as an occupation requiring "artistic skill."

And, TheFreeDicitionary.com mentions membership in a guild.

Between all three definitions we know that a 'craft' is a branch of a professional group or guild. It is a career or occupation, not simply a hobby.

Interestingly, there are various avenues that can be taken to become an accomplished or professional writer, but each one has the need for learning, practice, time, and commitment. Some writers may go to school and get degrees, others may learn from a coach or mentor, others from trial and error, failures and successes. But, whichever path is taken, there is a lot of work that goes into becoming experienced and knowledgeable in being a writer. As the saying goes, practice makes perfect.

But today, with the easy-to-do-it-yourself self-publishing explosion, writers may not be viewed as professionals. Certainly, most people have read a self-published book or ebook that lacks proper grammar, structure, and even clarity. These products are easy to spot, but yet they're available for sale, and the authors consider themselves writers.

While it's great that those who want to write have a vehicle to publish their own work, especially in this overwhelmed publishing market, those who don't take the time to learn the craft of writing do themselves and others an injustice. They make the self-publishing book market murky and the label of 'writer' less professional.

This shouldn't be the case.

Think of a professional musician. Imagine him playing an amazing piece, smooth, fluid, and beautiful – every note is perfect. Now imagine another musician; this one isn't in tune, can't read the music, misses notes, and sounds awful. Which musician do you want to be?

You should want to be the professional; the one who offers polished and experienced work; the one who earns a reputation for quality.

According to WritersHelper.com, it doesn't matter what your experience level is, there is always room for improvement. Writers should strive to "study ways to improve their craft." While this may take time and work, it is easy to find the needed help and resources.

To begin, do a search for online writing instruction; try the keyword "learn to write." You can also check your local schools for adult education classes, or take some college writing courses. There is an abundance of writing information available, much of it free or very inexpensive; take advantage of it.

Being a writer means you need to learn the **craft of writing,** and continue honing your skills.

The first step for a successful writing career is to write. But, simply writing isn't enough, the new writer will need to, as mentioned above, learn the craft of writing, along with the particular tricks of writing for children. Writing for children, in particular up to middle grade, is more complicated than other forms of writing. The reason is because you're dealing with children.

Rules, such as age-appropriate words, age-appropriate actions, age-appropriate topics, age-appropriate comprehension, storylines and formatting are all features that need to be tackled when writing for children.

Within the learning to write process, aside from reading books and magazines on the craft of writing, you will need to read, read, and read in the genre you want to write. Pay special attention to recently published books and their publishers. What works in these books? What type of style is the author using? What topics/storylines are publisher's publishing?

Dissect these books, and you might even write or type them word-for-word to get a feel for writing that works. This is a trick that writers new to copywriting use – you can trick your brain into knowing the right way to write for a particular genre or field. Well, not so much trick your brain as teach it by copying effective writing. Just remember, this is for the learning process only – you cannot use someone else's work, that's plagiarism.

Writing Goals, Detours, and Opportunity Cost

YOU'RE TAKING THE initiative by reading this book, but along with learning how to write, you need to remain focused on your writing goals. As you start your writing journey, hopefully you will take the time to think about and actually write out your **writing goals.**

This is a key element to seeing your goals recognized – you must write them down and keep them where you can see them every day. Certainly, you've heard this strategy before. It's simply not enough to think of your goals, you need to see them written and even visualize them.

Jack Canfield and his co-author Mark Victor Hansen of *Chicken Soup for the Soul* (http://chickensoup.com) wrote their goals out and pasted them everywhere possible, even in the bathroom. No matter where they were, they saw their objective and after 144 rejections, Chicken Soup for the Soul was finally accepted for publication.

Top article marketer Mark Thompson says, "Two of the vital ingredients for success online or in the "real world" is converting your Dreams to Goals and surrounding yourself with people with similar goals and ideals."

Again, this is achieved by making your writing goals visible, writing them down, and by projecting them. But, you also need to make your goals attainable. Don't overwhelm yourself with too many goals or unrealistic goals.

It's a good idea to limit your primary goals to no more than three. Under each goal list the strategies you'll take to achieve each one.

As an example, suppose you want to freelance for magazines. This is your number one goal and actions you might take to help you achieve that goal are:

1. Research three magazines you'd like to write for.
2. Decide on a topic that would be appropriate for each magazine.
3. Write an outline for the article.
4. Write a query letter for each magazine.
5. Submit to each magazine.

Then you would simply follow your own goal reaching instructions to obtain your objective/s.

One big pitfall or roadblock to achieving your writing goals though, aside from not writing them out and reviewing them every day, is a lack of focus and allowing yourself to get sidetracked by taking detours.

If you're like me you start the year with your goals front and center. Then you seem to get sidetracked doing 'this and that.'

You might decide it's a great idea to prepare and present workshops or webinars to build your mailing list or sell products. Or, you attended a number of webinars that told you how easy it is to make money creating your own information products. So, off you go, doing 'this and that.'

Unfortunately, unless the 'this and that' is earning you money, the detour is pointless. It's not only pointless, it creates an opportunity cost.

What do I mean by 'opportunity cost?'

If you spend your time and energy on projects that aren't in line with your end objectives (your writing goals), and those detour projects aren't earning you money, you've lost time and energy. And you've lost the money you might have made if you stuck to your original objectives.

BusinessDictionary.com defines 'opportunity cost' as "a benefit, profit, or value of something that must be given up to acquire or achieve something else."

That time, energy, and money you lost on your detours is the 'opportunity cost.'

If you do decide to make a detour, be sure the benefits (money, networking, learning, etc.) are worth it.

Achieving your goals takes discipline, drive, and perseverance. Don't let unfruitful detours derail your writing goals.

Section Five Assignment

- - - - - - - - - - - - -

1. CONTINUING WITH the short story or picture book you've been writing, add an ending. Your story should be within 1250 words, five pages.

Read your story carefully and write down any promises, hints, or subplots you developed. Make sure your ending is neatly tied up.

Also, check to see if your protagonist has grown in a visible manner. Has he become the hero? Will the reader recognize his growth?

Is there a take-away value to the story? If so, what is it?

2. After you do this assignment, read it and check for relevancy and clarity.

- Is the ending understandable?
- Is the overall story engaging?
- Will the reader find the ending satisfying?

If possible have a family member or friend read it to get a fresh viewpoint.

If you've had trouble with the last few lessons and haven't been able to come up with a story idea, check out a few folktales or classics and try rewriting one.

Section
Six

How to Revise and Edit, Research and Find a Publisher

DID YOU GIVE *any foreshadowing in the beginning? Did you pose any questions to the reader? This is the part of the story where you need to make sure you have answered each foreshadow and answer any questions a reader may have had with a satisfying ending. Again, leaving a reader with a 'huh?' feeling risks the chance of them never picking up another book from you again.*

Section Six Content:

Introduction to Lesson Six

Revisions and Editing
   Ten Tips Checklist for Self-editing
   Final Stages of Self-editing
   Five Writing Exercises
   Exercise Answers
   A Guide to Hiring a Freelance Editor
   The Manuscript's Finishing Touches
   Researching Publishers and Submissions
   A Bit About Self-Publishing: Before You Self-Publish
   Aim for Writing Success and Persevere
   Lesson Six Resources
   Lesson Six Assignment

Introduction to Section Six

IN A HIGHLIGHTS Foundation article, "Revisions is Where the Story Lives," it offers several quotes from top authors and editors. The first, and what the article title is based on, is from editorial consultant Eileen Robinson, "Revision is where the story lives."

This is to emphasis the importance of this section.

You might think having written a story with all the elements mentioned in this book was tough. Well, writing can be hard, but now comes the first roll-up your sleeves and dig in part . . . revisions and editing.

On these pages you'll pick your story apart, you'll learn about tight writing and some proper formatting, and lots of other stuff. We'll also go over how to research the right market for your books.

First up is revisions and editing.

Interestingly, most new writers think once their first draft is done they have a great book.

The first draft of your story is just that, a draft. It's by no stretch of the imagination the finished product. This is the 'releasing' or 'freeing' part – your vision is now on paper.

So, how do you get from your first draft to a polished manuscript that's ready to be submitted to publishers and/or agents?

Revisions and editing and more revisions and editing and . . .

You might think of this stage of writing like a potter and his lump of clay, or a sculptor. You may have the basic shape and details done, but now you need to chisel away the excess and fine tune the piece.

To start this process, you'll need to carefully read your manuscript. Not just read it, but be sure to read every word. What usually happens when you, the writer, are working on your own work is you're too close to it. You know what's intended. This causes a gap in your 'reading and actually seeing' ability. You end up 'not really' reading what's written – you're ahead of yourself, reading what you think is written . . . you see what you intended to write.

One strategy to help with this is to put your draft away for a few days to a couple of weeks. It'll help you see if fresher.

More importantly, this is where a critique group, one that has both new and experienced authors in it, becomes necessary, or at the very least have an experienced writing partner to go over your manuscript.

I can't emphasize enough the importance of getting your manuscript critiqued. It's actually a good idea to do this while you're in the process of writing it. Your critique partners' views and ideas can help you as you go along.

Okay, let me stop here a minute. Just as every writer has his own process of writing, this is true of how each one edits and revises his work.

Some writers may do this on a chapter basis, and then do an overhaul at the end. Other writers may write the complete draft and then begin revisions and edits. There are no set-in-stone rules for this process. You will need to develop your own method – the one you're most comfortable with.

If you do go for the chapter-by-chapter approach, you'll also need to do 'full' revisions. While revising and editing in bits and pieces may feel comfortable, you won't get the 'bird's eye view' of your manuscript. You won't 'get' how each chapter flows into the next or whether the overall story is coherent with each scene moving the story forward.

So, be sure to keep this in mind when approaching your revision process.

Cheryl Klein suggests setting a deadline for each phase of your revision process. Once you complete one phase give yourself a 'pat on the back.' She also recommends, working "large to small." This means working on the story structure and getting it right before working on the grammar, formatting, and proofing. "It's no good getting the dialogue pitch-perfect in a scene at one stage if you discover you need to delete the scene later" (*Second Sight*, 299).

Also, this section will talk about writing tight – don't use 10 words when you can use five. Writing tight is absolutely necessary. Another facet of revisions is you may realize a section or sentence just doesn't work and needs to be cut. This is what revisions are for, BUT, **if you cut sentences or paragraphs, don't delete them. Save them in a "cut" Word doc file.** You never know if you will end up wanting to retrieve something or use it for another project. Better safe than sorry.

From this point forward, the explanations will be based on a completed draft, but you can use the information for any process you choose.

Revisions and Editing

You have a competed draft in front of you and you need to get it polished to a shine. What's the first step?

The very first step is to put the draft away for a few days or even weeks. If you try to start revisions and editing after you just finish the draft, you'll miss too much. You need to give you and your draft some distance, so you can see it in a fresh light.

After the break, you'll need to read the manuscript CAREFULLY. You'll be looking at everything: story structure, coherency, the characters, continuity, the ending, along with overuse of certain words, excess words, and so on. We'll start with structural revisions.

REVISIONS:

It's now that you should notice if you mentioned in Chapter One that your protagonist has an injury on his left leg and then in Chapter Seven his injury is on his right leg, and all the other big and small errors or newbie mistakes.

When thinking about revisions, in the article "Revision Is a State of Mind," agent <u>Mary Kole</u> says, "Every scene needs to teach us something new about a character or plot element. Every chapter needs to further the plot along. Each plot and subplot needs to have an arc and resolve itself by the end. Characters, no matter how big or small, need to make some kind of change or progress. Emotions have to rise and fall like waves throughout."

It's now that you should notice what's wrong with the story and what's right. Here are some elements to look for:

- Do you have a 'grabbing' beginning?
- Does the beginning convey an inciting incident?
- Are your characters life-like?
- Are the characters' motives clear?
- Does your protagonist create an emotional link to the reader; is he engaging?
- Are your characters fully developed?
- Do you have an engaging antagonist?
- Does the middle reveal the full conflict?
- Do you have at least three obstacles that must be overcome?
- Is your protagonist the one who finds the solution to the conflict?
- Are there consequences for the characters' actions? Are the stakes known?
- Does your protagonist grow significantly by the end of the story?
- Is the dialogue realistic and helping to move the story forward?
- Have you primarily used showing, rather than telling?
- Do your chapter endings pull the reader into the next chapter?
- Does each scene move the plot forward?
- Does the story move forward?
- Is the story's plot and tension effective?
- Have you included description and setting?
- Is the story coherent?
- Is the story engaging?
- Is there an emotional tug in the story?
- Is the story arc's peak effective?
- Does the ending meet all the criteria for a 'good' ending?

- Can you recognize the story's theme?
- What's the takeaway value of the story?

Take in everything. And, reread the lessons to keep focused on how a story is constructed.

As you read your draft, take notes. According to Klein, "Resist the urge to start revising the actual writing now" (Second Sight, 296).

Your object at this point is to get a view of the overall picture. Include areas you think are 'bad' and areas you think are 'good.' This is also the time for writing down new thoughts and ideas you can weave into your manuscript.

You'll also want to make a list of each action and emotional event in the story. It's advisable to number these scenes, just in case you want to move them around. It'll help you keep track of everything. This is called bookmapping.

Along with this, in your character sheets/interviews you should include each significant character's initial motive for his/her actions, the obstacles in the way, and how they are overcome.

Klein also suggests listing the first ten bits of dialogue each significant character says. The idea behind this is to view the dialogue out of the frame of the story. Does the dialogue reveal who the character is? Does the character seem interesting based on the dialogue alone? Does the dialogue move the story forward? Will it make a connection with the reader?

After you've fully reviewed the manuscript and make the necessary lists mentioned above, you can start applying the changes you deem necessary.

As you're in revisions, occasionally put the draft away. Yes, this is necessary.

In her article, "Some Thoughts on Revision," Kole says, "In essence, you have to revise more than you think. Then put it away. Then come back to it in three months and revise again. I find writers often have the problem of too little revision, not too much."

While Kole says to put it away for three months, it depends on the author. Some writers need that distance to be able to read the manuscript with 'fresh' eyes. Others may not need as much time. But, you should now realize that revisions can be, in fact usually are, an on-going process. There are authors who take years to revise a draft.

In another article on revisions, "How Much Revision is Normal?," Kole explained that editors and agents are looking for highly polished manuscripts. They won't accept a manuscript that looks like its revisions were rushed or not thorough.

Critique groups help tremendously in this area, so take the time and put forth the effort to belong to a 'good' critique group.

Having read and now analyzing some traditionally published books in the genre you're writing should give you further insight into how a story is structured and carried out. These books will help you hone your craft and revise your story.

Okay, so at this point you definitely understand how essential revisions are. And, along with finding and fixing the story's structural weaknesses, what else needs to be addressed? Editing and proofreading.

EDITING ESSENTIALS:

The idea of editing is to eliminate all the non-essentials in your story. This is called 'tight writing.'

Quoting from the article "Revisions is a State of Mind" again, Kole says, "Each sentence needs to earn its keep in your writing and justify staying in the draft."

Along with this, the editing process checks for proper grammar, showing, formatting, and a number of other elements, some of which includes:

- Finding and eliminating excess, unneeded words
- Finding and eliminating unnecessary adverbs and adjectives
- Finding and eliminating overused words, such as 'was'
- Checking for misspelled words

- Making sure strong verbs are used
- Making sure you have varying sentence lengths
- Checking for age appropriate theme, suggestions, words, etc.

The following pages will go into editing details and give some writing/editing exercises.

Ten Tips Checklist for Self-editing

AFTER YOU'VE WRITTEN your story, had it critiqued numerous times, and revised it numerous times, it's time to proofread and self-edit. Be sure to take all precautions so you don't meet any obstacles on your road to publication.

On to the checklist:

1. Check for clarity

Check each sentence for clarity. It's important to remember that you may know what you intend to convey, but your readers may not. It'd be a good idea to have someone else read the manuscript for you. This is where a good critique group comes in handy.

2. Check for "telling" and over-worded sentences

Check each sentence for telling. You want to have "showing," not "telling."

Example: Joe hit his head and was dazed.

Alternative: Joe ran into the tree, head first. He wobbled a moment and fell to the ground.

Show, don't tell. Use your imagination and picture your character going through motions—maybe he's turning his lip up or he's cocking his head. Try to visualize it; this will help in showing rather than telling.

A good way to add more showing is to add more sensory details. Use the five senses to create a living character and breathe life into your story.

Example: Joe felt cold.
Alternative: A chill ran through Joe's body.

Example: Joe was frightened.
Alternative: Joe's breath stopped. Goosebumps sprung hair on his arms to attention.

3. Point of View: Watch for head hopping

This is especially important for young children's writers since their stories should be told from the protagonist's point of view or perspective.

If the story is being told from your main character's point of view (POV) make sure it stays there. If your POV character Joe is sad and wearing a frown, you shouldn't say: *Noticing his sad face Fran immediately knew Joe was distraught.* (This is bringing Fran's POV into the picture.)

You might say: *They were friends for so long Joe knew Fran would immediately notice his despair.*

Or, you can just use dialogue: "Joe, what's wrong?"

4. Watch for story consistency, conflict, and flow

Children need a structured story that is easy enough for them to understand. And, children need action and conflict to keep them engaged. A flow or rhythm should keep the story moving forward.

It's important to note that the conflict doesn't have to be an external edge-of-your-seat type of conflict; it can be an internal struggle.

For young children predictive and repetitive conflict works well, as in *Caps for Sale* and *Stephanie's Ponytail* mentioned earlier.

In regard to conflict, the article "Powerful Writing Tips" by Margot Finke explains, "The best manuscripts have a single dramatic question: Will Ahab catch the whale? Will the Jackal kill his target? Will the young lawyer escape the corrupt law firm that hired him? The twists and turns in your novel can (and should!) be intricate, but your foundation needs to have a sole, central conflict around which all the action revolves. A good way to test your manuscript is to synopsize your plot in a single sentence. Can you do it?"

Using *Walking Through Walls* as an example, the single dramatic question would be: Does Wang learn magic and if he does, will he use it for evil?

5. Use spell-check

Make sure you write with spell-check on or use your word processor's spell-check when you're finished with your manuscript. I like writing with it on.

Just be careful here because spell-check will catch misspelled words, but it won't catch words that are spelled correct, but are the incorrect word in regard to meaning.

<u>Example</u>: He was to tired.
<u>Correct</u>: He was too tired.

These words are called homonyms and spell-check will not catch them.

Other homonyms: hare/here/hair; bare/bear/; pear/pare/pair; stationary/stationery; peek/peak; principle/principal; capital/capitol; compliments/complements; cite/site/sight.

6. Use your Find function on your word processor

This is a great tool to check for "ly" words, "ing" words, weak verbs, and over used words such as "was."

7. Watch for redundancy

Check the story for repeated phrasing and even paragraph beginnings. You may not realize how many sentences you're beginning with "the" or "he." It's important to pay attention to these things.

8. Check for tight writing

In today's market, tight writing is important—readers have a shorter attention span. So, get rid of unnecessary words, text, and unnecessary dialogue tags.

Example: Joe had a really hard time lifting the very heavy and big trunk.
Alternative: Joe struggled to lift the huge trunk.

Also, watch for words such as "began" and "started."

Example: He began to lift the trunk.
Alternative: He lifted the trunk.

Larry Brooks says to put a "cap on overwriting and an addiction to adjectives and adverbs" (*Story Engineering*, 254).

9. Check for punctuation and grammar

There are a number of great books and even online articles that will help you learn proper punctuation and grammar. **I have some helpful links in this les-**

son's Resources page and in the Resources and Tools section in the Bonus Section. You can also do a Google search.

10. Children's writers: Take illustrations into account

When writing a picture book you need to allow for illustrations. Picture books are a marriage between content and illustrations—a 50/50 deal. So, watch for text that an illustration can handle. With picture books your content doesn't have to describe every little detail—the illustrations will embellish the story.

Final Stages of Self-editing

Okay, your revisions are done and so is your self-editing, or so you think. There is so much involved in self-editing, the lists and checkpoints can fill a book or more. So, I've included these additional steps for you to give the manuscript a final review and help catch some of what you missed.

1. Read your manuscript

Read it again. Try to read it slow and watch for all the self-editing tips you've learned and think you've applied. Spotting one's own errors is difficult since we know what we wrote and intended. Some of the other tips here will help with this problem.

2. Change the font and read it again.

Surprisingly, you will spot errors you just glazed over before. You won't run through it the same way you did with the original font.

3. Read each paragraph from the last sentence to the first

This is an interesting method for an additional self-edit. It's helpful because your brain won't be on auto-pilot. You will spot glitches within sentences that you would glaze over when reading normally.

Note: I don't mean reading each sentence backward; read each sentence as you would normally, but read the last sentence first and work your way to the beginning of the paragraph.

4. Print your manuscript

Okay, I know what you environmentalists are thinking . . . I'm one also. I try very hard not to waste paper in order to protect and save our trees. But, there is a difference between reading on a computer and reading paper copy. I don't know why our brain perceives it differently, it just does.

As you're reading your story, use a colored pen or pencil and mark the text you find errors in. Once you finish, go back to your computer document and correct the errors.

The other good aspect of this process is it's a good idea to have a hard copy of your manuscript near its final stage. **Unless you have an offsite backup, you can't be too careful** (I'd be skeptical of an offsite backup also – you never know with any online system). I've lost a number of files when my computer broke. And, I've even lost files on zip drives when the drives failed. So, from experience I'm gun-shy when it comes to saving my work.

If you do actually utilize Step 4 and print your story, be sure to recycle it if you no longer need that copy. I reuse paper I'm not going to save by using the back for notes, or giving it to my grandkids to color on. When I'm finished with the sheet, I either rip it into pieces or shred it then recycle it.

5. Check formatting

Now it's time to check the formatting of the manuscript.

Are the first lines of all the paragraphs indented with proper punctuation?

Does each new speaker have a new paragraph?

Did you use the Show/Hide function in your word processor to check the inner workings? For instance, years ago the proper spacing between sentences was two spaces. Now, the protocol is one space between sentences. The Show/Hide function displays a dot for each space.

Is your manuscript double spaced?

Did you use the correct formatting and punctuation for dialogue?

6. Get your manuscript edited

When you think it's perfect, have it edited by a professional before you start submitting it. Yeah, yeah, yeah, I know, you think this step is overkill and it will cost money. You're right on the second part, it will cost money, but it will be money well spent. If at all possible, try to make this step a part of your writing budget.

No matter how many times you self-edit, and how many times your critique group goes over your manuscript, there will be errors. Ask around for a reputable editor.

For a bit more information on having your manuscript edited, read "A Guide to Hiring a Freelance Editor," after the Exercises.

If you just can't afford it, be especially careful with your self-editing and critique process.

Five Writing Exercises

PROPER PUNCTUATION, GRAMMAR (including spelling), and More

There are a number of new writers who don't understand the importance of proper punctuation, grammar, and formatting. Put another way, they don't take the time to learn the basics of their craft.

Without taking the necessary steps, your manuscript will end up in the editor's trash pile. You could have a wonderful and engaging story, but if it lacks the basics, an editor or agent won't take the trouble to read it.

You may think it's the story that counts, but you'd be thinking wrong.

With all the manuscripts publishers and agents get, they don't have to bother with authors who don't take the time to learn the fundamentals of writing. In fact, they might even get annoyed that you'd bother sending it in.

This is just as true, if not more so, for self-publishing. You may be by-passing the publishers' or agents' gatekeepers, but you won't fool your readers. And, keep in mind that you'll be looking for reviews for your book. How do you think those reviews will read it you don't properly revise and edit your manuscript before publishing?

Below are five exercises; please review them all before starting.

The exercises consist primarily of dialogue quotations, simple punctuation, formatting, and spelling.

The answers can be found after the exercises.

EXERCISE ONE:

Edit the four sets of sentences below:

There are misspelled words, dialogue punctuation problems as well as improper sentence punctuation and format. Do your best to find and correct the errors.

John through the ball so high it hit the ceiling. Hey john what are you doing. You could brake something and my father would get really, really mad. Awh, don't worry Pete its just a nerf ball.

All dialogue:
Mary wood you pass me the potatoes. Suure Sue here you go. Do you want gravee to.

Dialogue:
Your very strong.

Main character's thoughts:
Boy, I should have brought something to eat with me. Who knew it'd take so long to cut this grass.

EXERCISE TWO:

In order to write with an eye to description and using showing rather than tell-ing, seeing things from a different viewpoint can be helpful. Using similes and metaphors will help you as a writer to see sentences and events in your story in a different light.

This exercise is to picture the following objects and write two similes and two metaphors for each:

1. A full moon
2. A desert
3. A rose in full bloom
4. A storm
5. A baby

Below are the descriptions of both the simile and metaphor. And, don't worry, this isn't a test, it's just to get you thinking about descriptions. Try to avoid the obvious choices such as for a baby, *he's cute as a button.*

A simile, according to ...*As One Mad With Wine and Other Similes,* is:

The simile is, of course, much more than an attention getter. It colors and clar-ifies ideas by comparing two dissimilar things and does so in a straightforward way by introducing the comparison with the word **like** or **as**—or sometimes with the phrases **as if, as though, is comparable to, can be likened to, akin to, similar to.** This directness makes the simile the most accessible of all figures of speech, a favorite device for both literary and ordinary self-expression.

Examples:

Cold as a miser's heart –*Donald Seaman*
Close as two peas in a pod –*H. I. Phillips*

A metaphor, according to *Metaphors Dictionary* is:

Whether poetic or colloquial, simple or complex, a metaphor compares two unlike objects or ideas and illuminates the similarities between them. It accomplishes in a word or phrase what could otherwise be expressed only in many words, if at all.

Examples:

My cup runneth over –The Bible, O.T., Psalms 23:5
You are the salt of the earth –The Bible, N.T., Matthew 5:13
An old man is life's parody –*Simone de Beauvoir, The Coming of Age*
Power is poison –*Henry Adams, The Education of Henry Adams*

EXERCISE THREE:

Another common problem that new writers encounter is showing rather than telling.

Rewrite the following 'telling' sentences using as many of the five senses you can: sight, hearing, smell, taste, and touch. *Remember, 'showing' is conveyed through action, dialogue, and sensory description.*

1. The beach is hot.
2. I have a lot of homework.
3. He's the worse player on the team.
4. The mall was crowded.
5. That was the best pizza I ever had.

Examples for number one above:

- The ice cream melted faster than Jimmy could lick it.
- The sun melted the plastic lunch bag left lying on the blanket.

- Pete looked at the sand then at the waves curling up on the shore. Sweat dripped from his forehead and the back of his neck. He stepped off the blanket and hopped from foot to foot until he reached the water.

EXERCISE FOUR:

New writers of children's stories often forget that the point-of-view (POV) must be that of the main character/protagonist. The story must be described/shown through the main character's five senses.

In a post by Mary Kole at KidLit.com (http://kidlit.com/2009/12/23/voice-loud-and-clear/) POV or voice is explained:

Here are two ways of describing the exact same thing: a green couch. First: "It was a moss-green item of furniture that could fit four people." Second: "The lumpy old raft of a couch was baby-poop-green and threatening to make me sick. After all, it was jammed with my three least-favorite people: Uncle Mordy, Aunt Mildred, and my creepy cousin Kenny. Oh yeah... and me."

For children's stories, especially for young children, the POV must be singular. The story must be told through the dialogue, actions, and sensory description of the main character.

In the text below, the main character for this exercise is Tommy. Which POV is correct?

1. Tommy dug his cleats in. He raised the bat to his shoulder. A second later he watched the ball heading toward him . . . like a torpedo out of it tube. Without blinking he swung the bat. CRRAACCK. Stunned, he dropped the bat and ran. *Did . . . did I just hit the ball.*

2. "Pete! Did you see that? I didn't think he'd hit that ball—it came so fast," said Jim as he threw a pretend pitch.

3. Pete couldn't believe Tommy hit that ball. "How'd he do that? He's the worse player on the team."

EXERCISE FIVE:

Write a short story, or beginning of a story, incorporating: showing, point of view, and correct dialogue punctuation as well as formatting.

Use the information from this book and look at the tips below to help you with this exercise.

The subtitles to "10 Fiction Pitfalls" by Sam McCarver, in the May2010 issue of *The Writer* are:

1. Don't put extensive back-story in your first pages
2. Similarly, don't let narration dominate your story as a whole
3. Don't lose control over your plot
4. Eliminate weak dialogue
5. Don't label characters
6. Don't write a 'simple' plot
7. Don't talk directly to the reader
8. Don't write in the passive voice
9. Don't submit manuscripts in nontraditional formats
10. Don't overlook the value of good writing style

Now, we'll break each one down:

1. Your beginning needs to be action filled. Weave the back-story in small pieces throughout the story.

2. The same goes with narration. I began my children's fantasy chapter book with two paragraphs of narration. Fortunately, the editor who looked at my book saw past my faux pas. I was told to change it to action and dialogue and work the narration in other ways. According to the article mentioned above: "A story should consist of one scene following another, connected by narration [. . .]. Show it visually—in scenes."

3. Begin with a detailed outline and work from it. You can always change it as you go along, but it will be your GPS throughout the story.

4. Watch for "he said," she said" words. Having a dialogue tag is not always necessary.

 Action and sensory description should dictate who is speaking and show what is happening. If a dialogue tag can be omitted, be sure to omit it.

5. Watch for weak adjectives, words such as: beautiful, smart, handsome, strong, old, tall, and funny. Use description (descriptive detail) to show how they look or act.

6. "To solidify your plot, answer the six journalistic questions: Who? What? When? Where? Why? And How?" See the article "Writing a Hot Plot" link on the Resources page.

7. This is, in my opinion, common sense. You wouldn't say within your story: "Now, you readers see what I'm talking about? She just doesn't want to marry the prince."

8. We're back to showing with dialogue, action, sensory description, and strong verbs. Watch for words such as: was, were, had, is, and are. You should also check those "ly" words. See the example in Exercise 3.

9. Make sure your manuscript is properly formatted:

- It should be double spaced.

- The first sentence of each paragraph should be indented.

- Each new character speaking gets his own paragraph—create a new paragraph each time the speaker changes.

10. Use details: Switch up the sentence structures; have long, mid, and short sentences. Short sentences can show that the pace is picking up. Also use different sentence styles. Use description and imagery. Be sure to show, not tell.

The answers to the exercises begin on the next page.

Exercise Answers

EXERCISE ONE:

You were to edit the four sentences below:

SENTENCE ONE: John through the ball with all his might and it hit the ceiling. Hey john what are you doing. You could brake something and my father would get really, really mad. Awh, don't worry Pete, its just a nerf ball.

<u>FIX:</u>

John threw the ball with all his might.

"Hey John, what are you doing? My father will ground me if you break something."

"Awh, don't worry Pete. It's just a nerf ball."

You can notice there are a few changes:

<u>DETAILS:</u>

1. "hit the ceiling" was eliminated.
   a. Eliminating unnecessary words tightened the sentence.
   b. Now there is room for the illustrator to *paint a picture*, if this were a picture book.
2. Correct spelling of "threw," "break," and "it's."
3. Correct formatting and punctuation.
4. Reworded a bit for tighter writing.

Each new character speaking gets his own paragraph—create a new paragraph each time the speaker changes. And in manuscripts, the first line of each paragraph is indented.

SENTENCE TWO: Mary wood you pass me the potatoes. Suure Sue here you go. Do you want gravee to.

<u>FIX:</u>

"Mary, would you pass the potatoes?"

"Sure, here you go. Do you want gravy too?"

(The two sentences above should be indented for new paragraphs)

<u>DETAILS</u>

1. Correct spelling of: would, sure, gravy, and too.
2. Corrected the formatting and punctuation.
3. Eliminated Sue's name. Depending on the paragraph or surrounding content, you may need to include a tag, but if you can (if the content clearly shows who is being addressed) do not add the person's name. It's not a natural way of speaking—you would not reference the person's name you are speaking to unless you were trying to get his attention.

SENTENCE THREE: Your very strong.

FIX:

"You're very strong." You might also want a stronger adverb than 'very.' Possibly: You're super-strong. OR: You're strong like Superman.

DETAILS:

1. Correct spelling of "you're."
2. Correct formatting and punctuation.

SENTENCE FOUR: Boy, I should have brought something to eat with me.

FIX:

I should have brought something to eat.

DETAILS:

1. Text is in italics because it's internal dialog, thoughts.
2. Eliminated "Boy." It's an unnecessary word.
2. Eliminated "with me." This is understood. Remember tight writing.

For children's writing it's appropriate to use italics for your character's internal dialogue.

EXERCISE FOUR:

You were to determine which POV was correct in the sentences below:

1. Tommy dug his cleats in. He raised the bat to his shoulder. A second later he watched the ball heading toward him . . . like a torpedo out of its tube. Without blinking he swung the bat. CRRAACCK. Stunned, he dropped the bat and ran.

DETAILS:

Tommy is the main character, so it's only through his senses that the story can be told. If Tommy can't see, hear, touch, taste, or smell it, it doesn't exist in the story.

This is what point of view (POV) or perspective is – for young children's stories, the story should be told through the main character's perspective.

While you can add more than one POV when you get to upper middle grade stories, you should make it very clear when the POV is changing. It might be a good idea to put different POVs in separate chapters in middle grade books. I would strongly advise limiting POVs to no more than two in an upper middle grade.

Clarity rules!

A Guide to Hiring a Freelance Editor

IF YOU'RE QUESTIONING why you need to have your manuscript profession-ally edited after going to the trouble of having it critiqued and working on it meticulously and endlessly, the answer is simple: An author and a critique group are not a match for the expert eyes of a professional editor.

Did you and your critique group catch all the punctuation errors? How about knowing when or if it is permissible to use quotation marks outside of dia-logue? Do you know about the Find function on your word program to check for over used words, such as *was* and *very*. What about ellipsis dots, or the over use of other adjectives and adverbs?

This is just the tip of the iceberg. Isn't it understandable why it's important to take that extra step, and expense, to have your manuscript edited. If you're un-decided, ask the professional writers you know if they recommend it. You can also ask if they could recommend a qualified and affordable editor.

The powers that be, editors, agents, reviewers, and publishers, all know the difference between a professionally edited manuscript and one that is not.

Every house needs a solid foundation, right? Getting your manuscript professional edited is the same thing - it will provide a solid foundation. The number of authors seeking publishers and/or agents is staggering. Yet, the number of publishers and agents is limited.

If you can afford it, give your manuscript every advantage possible. Having a professionally edited manuscript can be the deciding factor in whether your manuscript makes it to the editor's 'to read' pile or the trash pile.

Will hiring a freelance editor ensure you pitch the perfect game? In writing terms, will it ensure you get published?

No, but again, it will give your manuscript the best shot at acceptance.

Do you need an editor? If you can afford it, YES.

There are a number of pros and cons related to whether you should hire a freelance editor. Some writers benefit greatly from the experience while others have a difficult time and may even get insulted.

Four Points to Examine Before Hiring a Freelance Editor:

1. One of the most important aspects of hiring someone to critique or edit your work is to be open to criticism. If you do not have the personality to handle constructive criticism, suggestions, and/or edits, then you shouldn't hire a freelance editor.

2. Before you contemplate hiring a freelance editor, get your manuscript in the best shape possible. What this means is you should know your craft or be engaged in learning it.

You should obviously belong to a critique group that focuses on the genre you write. This group should have new and experienced/published authors in it. This will help you to hone your craft through the critiques you receive and the critiques you give.

Next up on the road to learning your craft is to join a couple of writing groups – again be sure they have new and experienced writers. You can even look into a writing coach or instructor.

3. Hiring a freelance editor to go over your manuscript will not guarantee publication, even the best in the field can't promise this. What an experienced editor will do is help you to get it in the best shape possible. But, whether or not you take his/her advice is another story. And, again, even if you do, there are no guarantees.

This holds true everywhere in the writing world. You may send your manuscript out, after it's polished, to 30, 50, or more publishers and agents and get rejections. Then, you send it to one more and it happens this publisher has been looking for what you have. Time and Chance, my friends, Time and Chance.

But, it's a sure bet if your manuscript isn't polished, you won't ever get that far.

4. If you did your best to get your manuscript into what you think is publishable shape and you want an editor to give it a final once over, be sure to ask for recommendations from other writers.

The Manuscript's Finishing Touches

Congratulations, you have a finished and polished manuscript - one ready for submissions.

But, before you send it off, there are a couple of things you need to do first. While they don't involve touching the manuscript itself, they are needed to get the manuscript moving into the right hands.

1. Create a logline and elevator pitch

A log line or pitch line is a one sentence description or your manuscript. This may take a bit of trial and error, but it's important to master.

This is also called you elevator pitch, or simply your pitch. It's a very condensed yet concise description of your story. It can be one to several sentences long (one is better though).

The idea is to grab the publisher, editor, or agent's attention and interest with the core of your story in the span of under 3 minutes.

The marketing arena's idea of the pitch is a one sentence calling card – you're unique selling proposal or proposition.

The idea behind the elevator pitch is to imagine that you get on an elevator and surprisingly you're there with a potential client, or in the case of writing for children or writing in general, a publisher or agent. You are given just the time for the elevator ride, which is approximated at 3 minutes, to pitch your story. That's the elevator pitch.

It may also happen that the time you have to pitch your manuscript may be under a minute. Suppose you're at a conference and happen to get on the elevator at the end of the day with a frazzled publisher or agent. You want that very short span of pitching time to be as effective as you can make it, without annoying or further frazzling your target. It may be the only opportunity you'll have for a direct, although very brief, uninterrupted pitch.

The one sentence pitch takes time, effort, and a lot of practice. You need to condense your entire manuscript into one sentence. Within that sentence you need to harness the *soul* of your story in a simple, concise, and hooking pitch.

The general writing consensus is to do your best and create one sentence that tells what your story is about. Once you have it nailed, expand it into a few more, adding only the most important aspects of the story. This is excellent practice for tight writing.

This way you'll have two different versions of a micro pitch. It's important to always be prepared – you never know when or where you may come upon an unsuspecting publisher or agent . . . maybe you'll have a few seconds, maybe you'll have 3 minutes.

Here is an example of a one sentence pitch from RockWayPress.com (1):

Two brothers and their female cousin decide to track down a serial killer themselves, not realizing that one of them may be the very killer they seek.

Here's another one from the blog at Buried in the Slush Pile (2):

The Emerald Tablet -- In this midgrade science fiction novel, a telepathic boy discovers that he is not really human but a whole different species and that he must save a sunken continent hidden under the ocean.

And, here's my own one sentence pitch for my children's fantasy chapter book. The 99 word version hooked a contract with a publisher:

Children 7-10 love fantasy and magic and *Walking Through Walls* has just that. Twelve-year-old Wang decides he'll be rich and powerful if he can become a mystical Eternal.

Obviously, if you have a scheduled pitch with an agent or publisher, you will need to adhere to the publisher or agent's rules. You may be able to provide a pitch with 100-200 words. But, it's a good idea to have that one sentence pitch on hand for that you-never-know moment.

TIP: Have your pitch on your business cards. And yes, as an author you should have business cards.

~~~~~~

Material cited:

(1) http://www.rockwaypress.com/one_sentence_pitch.htm (Sorry, link no longer works)
(2) http://cbaybooks.blogspot.com/2008/04/one-sentence-pitch.html

2. Create a synopsis

A synopsis is a short description of your story. Be sure your writing is tight and focused; leave out the fluff. The content should be, at the very least, meticulously self-edited and proofread before sending it off to an agent or publisher. You are trying to grab the reader's attention and let the reader know that you are grammar literate.

Basically, the synopsis should briefly let the editor know what the book is about: the beginning of your story, your main character's needs or wants, how he strives to reach his goals, the obstacles/conflicts in his way, and how he overcomes the conflicts and moves forward to the final outcome (yes, you give the ending away in this case).

I read an interesting article recommending that your synopsis be created using your detailed outline as a foundation.

3. Create a query letter

A query is a sales pitch. It should be three to six paragraphs and on only ONE page.

The first paragraph quickly and interestingly describes the story; it's the hook. Include the genre and word count.

The second and third paragraphs (if you have more than three) can elaborate on the story itself.

The next to last paragraph you can tell a bit about you, your qualifications for writing the book. And if you're a savvy marketer, it's a good idea to include a bit on how you intend to help market the book and what published books are in your genre.

The final paragraph is the conclusion: thank the person for his/her time; you might mention whether the submission is a simultaneous one. Keep it short.

Other things to keep in mind:

- The query should be single-spaced with a 'normal' 12 PT font (Arial, Veranda, Calibri, Times New Roman) .

- If at all possible, personalize the letter in the first paragraph. Maybe you read an article by the agent or editor in which he mentioned he was looking for manuscripts in the genre you write. Or, maybe you saw/met a publisher at a conference.

- In the first paragraph you should include your protagonist and the conflict.
- Make the hook quick and easy – don't get into details.
- Keep your hook paragraph between 100 and 200 words.

- In regard to your bio, if it doesn't put anything on the table, leave it out. If you're an unpublished, unknown individual with no credible reasons for writing your book, leave the bio out.

According to Writer's Market 2017, "In many cases, it [the query letter] determines whether editors or agents will even read your manuscript. A good query makes a good first impression; a bad query earns a swift rejection."

And, READ the publisher's guidelines. Okay, that's not accurate–you need to STUDY and FOLLOW those guidelines precisely.

Items to watch for when reading the publisher's guidelines:

1. What genre does that particular publishing house or magazine publish?
2. Does the publisher accept simultaneous submissions? A simultaneous submission is when you are submitting the same manuscript, at the same time, to more than one publisher or agent.
3. Is there a specific word count involved?
4. Does the publishing house accept unagented queries?

These are only four items to watch out for, but there are more. So, we go back to the main rule for querying: FOLLOW the GUIDELINES!

Queries will be discussed in more detail under the Four Steps to Querying Publishers and Agents topic.

4. Final Step: Submissions

Okay, your manuscript is polished and shiny, now it's time to submit. But, hold on . . . as mentioned above, check each publisher's guidelines before you submit.

In fact, don't just check the guidelines, you need to study them, and follow them explicitly. If a publisher asks for submission by mail only, don't email your submission. If the word count on an article or story is up to 1000 words, don't submit a story with 1150 words.

Next, we'll look at researching publishers.

Researching Publishers and Submissions

Now, you're set. Off you go on your submissions fishing trip. But, don't just drop the line randomly; be sure you do research and find the best spot – one where you know the fish are biting.

What this means is to look for publishing houses that are best suited to your manuscript, and ones that are accepting submissions.

There are a number of groups and services you can take advantage of when researching publishers and/or agents.

The first step is to know what genre your story fits into. You don't want to submit a picture book to a publisher that deals with only young adult. Always research the publishers you're looking into.

Don't randomly submit a manuscript to a publisher or agent; again, study their guidelines. Most that accept picture book manuscripts will allow you to submit the entire manuscript. But, those that accept middle grade and young adult may request only three chapters.

Here are some generic tips for formatting and submitting a manuscript:

- Include a title page; it should include your name and contact information
- Manuscripts should be typed in a common typeface, such as Courier or Times New Roman and be in 12 PT font
- It should be double spaced
- The first sentence of each paragraph should be indented
- Each chapter beginning should be on a new page (use Page Break)
- In regard to dialogue, each new speaker gets a new paragraph
- You'll need to create a header with your name, the book title, and the page number
- Most publishers, especially the major ones use their own illustrators
- Illustration notes are usually frowned upon by publishers
- A cover letter must be included
- A SASE is usually required for a response
- Keep it simple and professional
- DO NOT query unless you have a completed and polished manuscript
- The publishing industry is overburdened, so expect to wait two to six months for a response

FINDING PUBLISHERS

Do the Research

You need to send your query to the right recipients. You can have the most professional looking query letter, but if you send a query to a romance publisher and you have written a children's picture book, guess what? You'll be out of luck.

Research for publishers and agents who work within the genre you write. There are services, such as **Writer's Market** that provide information on where and how to sell your articles or manuscripts. While these types of services may charge for their use, it is a worthwhile investment.

Here are other tools you can use to help find a publisher or agent:

Writer's Market (Book)
Provides book and magazine publisher and agent information

Children's Writer's and Illustrator's Market (Book)
Provides book and magazine publishers, and agents information, specifically for those writing for children

Writer's Market (Online)
http://writersmarket.com
Find places to sell your writing, whether you've got a book, manuscript, or article idea. Use information specific to your writing needs--whether you're interested in fiction, nonfiction, poetry, children's, scriptwriting, or agents--with their niche-specific pages.

Publisher's Marketplace
http://www.publishersmarketplace.com/
Track deals, sales, reviews, agents, editors, and publishing news

Guide to Literary Agents:
Where and How to Find the Right Agents to Represent Your Work
http://www.guidetoliteraryagents.com/blog/

Agent Query
http://www.agentquery.com/
A free, searchable database of agents with article and formatting tips

The Literary Marketplace
http://www.literarymarketplace.com/lmp/us/index_us.asp

If you choose to get the books listed above, rather than online options, you will need to get the newest versions each year. Agents and publishers are changing staff all the time. And, new companies are popping up and existing ones are closing down. You will need up-to-date information for your query submissions.

You can also find a tremendous amount of information on all aspects of writing children's fiction at the **Society of Children's Book Writers and Illustrators** (SCBWI).

As you're researching publishers and agents, make a list of those that are best suited to your book. Also, it's a good idea to check out the publishers' book listings. If they just published a book on a middle grade fantasy adventure, chances are they're not going to want to invest in a similar book. So, don't bother submitting to that particular company if that's what your book is about.

Be thorough in your research and be wise about your time and energy and that of the publisher and agents.

Writer's Market and Publisher's Marketplace list imprints and editors by name. They also provide a list of the books published. This is a very handy tool.

Again, read each publisher's or agent's guidelines carefully and follow them.

SUBMISSIONS

ONE MORE TIME: Before you think about submitting your work anywhere, be sure you've completed the necessary steps to learn the craft of writing. You're manuscript needs to be as polished as you can possibly get it.

Submissions can fall into two categories: those to publishers and those to agents. In regard to submitting to agents, in a webinar presented by Writer's Digest, agent Mary Kole advised to "research agents."

This means to find out what type of agent they are in regard to the genre they work with and the agent platform they provide: do they coddle their authors, do they crack the whip, are they aggressive, passive, involved, or complacent. Know what you're getting into before querying an agent, and especially before signing a contract.

The same advice works for submitting to publishers; research publishers before submitting to them. Know which genres of children's books they handle and the type of storylines they're looking for.

Whether submitting to a publisher or an agent, always follow the guidelines and always personalize the query. There may be times the guidelines do not provide the name of the editor to send the query to, but if you can find that information, use it.

According to Mary Kole, it's also important to know how to pitch your story. This entails finding the story's hook. Agents and publishers also want to know what the book's selling points will be and what successful books it's similar to. In addition, they will expect to be told what your marketing strategy will be, if you have one. It's a good idea to create an online presence and platform before you begin submissions; let the agents and publishers know you will actively market your book.

Along with the story's hook, you need to convey: who your main character is and what he/she is about; the action that drives the story; the main character's obstacle, and if the main character doesn't overcome the obstacle, what's at stake.

You'll also need to include the conclusion.

Kole recommends reading "the back of published books" to see how they briefly and effectively convey the essence of the story. This will give you an idea of how to create your own synopsis.

When querying, keep your pitch short and professional. And, keep your bio brief and relevant. You will need to grab the editor or agent and make them want to read your manuscript.

4 STEPS TO QUERYING PUBLISHERS & AGENTS

While some authors choose to send queries to a publisher or an agent, there is no reason to choose, send queries off to both. But, there are a few steps you need to be aware of before you actually start submitting:

1. First Impressions

Professionalism, professionalism, professionalism. Yes, be professional. As with any business correspondence, do not use colored stationary, colored text, elaborate font, scented paper or envelope, or any other unprofessional features.

You get one shot at making a first impression, don't blow it on silly additions. And, don't try to be cute or send a gift. Again, be professional.

2. Content

In the February 2011 issue of the Writer, agent Betsy Lerner explained, "Editors and agents alike enjoy nothing more than being startled awake by a witty or moving letter." They want to see something special and unique; this is where your pitch comes in.

While you may have taken heed and had your manuscript critiqued and looked at by an editor, you can do the same with your query letter.

You want to give the impression that you are intelligent, so your query letter must reflect that. Get it in the best shape possible, with a great hook, and then send it off to be critiqued.

Publishers and agents receive more queries than they can comfortably handle, so don't give them a reason to simply reject yours because of unprofessionalism. Give your query and manuscript every possible opportunity for success.

3. Make it personal

If at all possible address the query to the editor or agent by name. The online sources and books mentioned will usually have the name of the contact.

If there is a confusing name, such as only initial instead of a first name, don't assume the person is a man or woman (Mr. / Ms.). Address the editor/agent with the name as you see it.

And, if you can't find any information on who to address the query to, call the publishing house or agency and ask who to send it to. Make every attempt to get a name.

4. The query format

As mentioned earlier, the first paragraph is the introduction. It will have the title, genre, and word count.

The middle paragraphs are a brief synopsis of the story.

The last paragraph, or closing paragraph, provides a bit of information about you in regard to your qualifications and writing career.

At the bottom of your page, under your name, include your address, phone number, email address, and the URL to your website.

Finally, be sure to thank the editor or agent for his time and consideration.

You will submit your query along with the material required in the guidelines of each specific publisher or agent.

Is the publisher for real?

What I see happening more and more, is authors are searching online for publishers. Even when "traditional publishers" is put into a search box the results given will include self-publishing companies and hybrid-publishing companies.

You need to be careful. Read their About pages and if you're still not sure if they're really traditional, contact them and ask.

If you happened to submit and within a week to four weeks you get a letter of acceptance, see if it includes how much you have to pay for publishing your book.

IF you are asked for money, they are NOT a traditional publisher.

A Bit About Self-Publishing, Before You Jump In

WITH TODAY'S OVERSATURATED and tight publishing market, it's difficult to find even a small publisher for the manuscript you've slaved over.

Many authors have taken the matter into their own hands and are going the self-publishing route. This can be a worthwhile venture...if you first know a couple of things:

1. Self-publishing can cost you money

While spending money used to be an 'absolute' when venturing into the self-publishing world, it is not today. But, if you use a vanity press, a POD company, or a co-publishing company it will cost you.

How much money will depend on the company you choose and which of the various services they offer that you buy into. And, there will be many services offered aside from printing your book into a digital or physical format.

Additional services will include: editing, illustrations, cover design, copyright, distribution, press releases, promotion, and so on. Each of these additional services will cost you more money, although most of these companies do offer package deals.

I know writers who have spent under a thousand dollars and others who have spent well over five thousand dollars to publish a book.

In addition to this, selling books is a TOUGH business. Just because your book is in print or digitally available, it does not mean you will recoup your money, or make a profit.

It may sound a bit harsh, but there are writers who spend money on self-publishing hoping it will bring a return on their investment - this is not always the case.

You might look into the FREE or low-cost e-publishing options through services like Amazon KDP (Kindle), Lulu, Smashwords, Draft2Digital, and IngramSpark. But, be aware that it can be tricky to upload your cover and interior content exactly as specified. Plan on giving yourself enough time to figure things out.

Another option is to hire someone to upload your book onto Kindle.

In addition, services like Amazon's CreateSpace and IngramSpark will also publish a physical book at a minimal cost. They get a percentage of the book when sold, and you will have to set a minimum retail price – meaning you won't be able to set it lower. But, it's worth looking into.

2. Join a critique group before actually publishing

I've mentioned this before, but it warrants repeating.

When choosing a critique group, be sure there are new and experienced (preferably published) writers as members, and it needs to focus on the genre you write in.

In a critique group, you'll quickly begin to see, through critiques of your work and that of the other members, how writing should be done. You'll begin to spot grammatical and punctuation and storyline errors – you will begin to hone your craft. The group will help you polish your manuscript – you'll be amazed at the difference.

At this point, it is advisable to have it edited as a final insurance. Often, the company you go with to self-publish will offer editing services. Just price it compared to hiring your own editor. And, be very sure the company is not outsourcing their editing to less than professional people – this is very common in the self-publishing world.

3. Learn the craft of writing

Along with a critique group, it's important to join one or two writing groups. This will be a tool to begin your networking and it will also be a learning experience. Just in the messages alone, you'll pick up valuable tidbits of information. And, you can always ask questions.

Read and read and read. Read in the genre you are writing and read books on writing. This is where asking questions in your writing group will come in handy. Ask members for recommendations on books you should read to hone your craft.

If possible, take some writing workshops, classes or e-courses, and attend writing conferences. If you can't afford it, look for free online ones.

4. Research self-publishing companies

Whether you're looking at print-on-demand, full-service publishing companies, digital publishing companies, or hybrids, research a number of them before signing a contract. Along with finding out what services they offer and the cost, check into their reputation.

5. Learn about marketing

If you have a polished product to offer, and you should if you've taken your time and did it 'right,' you will need to focus on the marketing element of writing. They'll be more about this a bit later.

6. Don't be in a rush

Take your time and do it right. Ensure your book has every opportunity for success. Don't just jump in...it can be a very expensive splash!

NOTE: When referencing self-publishing, I'm talking about any venture in which you are paying to have your book published by a publishing/printing/distribution service, whether a POD, co-publisher, or companies such as BookBaby and Golden Box Books.

Here's an article on self-publishing you might find interesting:

Advice on Self-Publishing a Children's Book
https://www.janefriedman.com/self-publish-childrens/

Aim for Writing Success and Persevere

IT'S NOT NECESSARILY the best writer who gets published and has a successful writing career...it's the writer who perseveres. Writing can be a long and arduous road and is usually filled with a great deal of rejection. But, if you work toward your goal, learn your craft, and keep moving forward, you have what it takes to become published.

Writing success can mean different things to different writers. Some writers may simply want to get a book or article published; others may want to be on the New York Times Best Sellers List; still others may want to make a living writing; and there are those who may be seeking wealth and fame. The key here is to dig down and really know what your perception of writing success is.

Once you are certain what you are aiming for, take the necessary steps to become the writing success you dream of.

Sounds easy, right?

Well, we all know it's not. If it were, there would be no struggling writers.

The first problem we seem to run into is actually realizing how we perceive success, or what we want from our writing efforts. According to Jack Canfield, co-creator of *Chicken Soup for the Soul*, the number one reason for being stuck and not realizing your potential or goals is the lack of clarity.

Here are five steps to help you focus on your aim:

Step One: You Must Define Your Goals and Your Perception of Success

It's not sufficient to state you want to be a published writer; you need to proclaim the specifics. You want to be a self-help nonfiction author of published books and magazine articles earning an income of $100,000 per year. You can even get much more specific than that—the more specific your goals and intentions are the more likely you will attain them.

Step Two: Create a Plan

When you finally have a break through and know exactly what you want from your writing efforts, you need to prepare a detailed plan. Your plan, just like your goals, needs to be very specific.

Think of a recipe: You plan is to bake a cake, but you'll need more than just the ingredients, you'll need the exact amount of each ingredient, the proper procedure for mixing them together, the baking temperature, how long to bake it, how long to cool it before removing it from the pan . . . you get the idea.

Now you're on your way . . . you have specific goals . . . a detailed plan . . . but . . . you're still not achieving success.

Step Three: Take Action

Think of the first two steps as the foundation of your house. To move forward toward success, you need to build the house. This takes action; it actually takes more than just action, it takes ongoing action and perseverance to carry you through to completion.

Step Four: Projection

You have the other steps down pat, now picture yourself attaining your goals. According to motivational speakers, you will have a much greater chance of making it happen by projecting success. This step encompasses a number of strategies such as envisioning, projection, projection boards, and affirmations.

Step Five: Persevere

Jack Canfield and co-author Mark Victor Hansen had *Chicken Soup for the Soul* rejected 144 times before a publisher signed them on.

You can also check out the article below:

Determination, Focus, and Perseverance

http://karencioffiwritingforchildren.com/2016/06/05/writing-success-focus-determination-and-perseverance/

Remember, before you actually submit your fully edited and polished manuscript, you need to have a well-written query letter, a synopsis, and your logline.

Section Six Resources

HELPFUL ARTICLES

Writing a Hot Plot
http://kidlit.com/2009/12/09/writing-a-hot-plot/

Why You Don't Use "Suddenly"
http://kidlit.com/2009/08/27/why-you-dont-use-suddenly/

Tag, You're It! How To Write Excellent Dialogue Tags
http://kidlit.com/2009/06/02/how-to-write-dialogue-tags/

Pitchcraft
http://kidlit.com/2010/02/15/pitchcraft/

Punctuation Tips
http://www.lrcom.com/tips/punctuation.htm

Reductive Revision
http://kidlit.com/2009/04/10/reductive-revision/
Provides a great hands-on example of writing tight

Proofreading Tips from Philip Corbett Times Editor
http://topics.blogs.nytimes.com/2011/10/04/the-readers-lament/

You Finished Your Novel . . . Or Have You?
http://4rvreading-writingnewsletter.blogspot.com/2011/07/you-finished-your-novel-or-have-you.html

"THE END" is Only the Beginning:
A Step-by-Step Guide to Refining Your Manuscript
http://anitanolan.com/theend.html

The Stages of Editing (Humor)
http://margaretmcgaffeyfisk.com/the-stages-of-editing/

Section Six Assignment

DO THE EXERCISES in this lesson.

Review your story and complete a self-edit.

Create a logline (one sentence description) for your story.

Create a short synopsis of your story.

Create a long synopsis. The length of the long synopsis will depend on the length of your story. If it's a PB, a couple of paragraphs should be plenty. If it's a 100 or 200 page novel, your synopsis will need to be more substantial.

Follow the instructions in this lesson and make a list of appropriate publishers and agents you might want to submit to.

If you're self-publishing, make a list of services you can work with.

Now, put your manuscript away for a week or two, maybe a month or longer. Then proof and edit it again.

When you're sure it's as polished as it can be, you have two choices:

1. Ask around for a freelance editor to go over your story.

2. Self-edit it again, and again, until it's sparkly clean. Then submit it.

I've also included a separate bonus section that has additional children's writing advice and lots of resources.

Keep reading, learning, writing and submitting!

"It's not what you've done that matters – it's what you haven't done."

~ Mark Twain

Section Seven

From Contract to Editor to Sales

Your writing journey is far from over once your manuscript is polished and you begin submissions. Once a publisher or agent accepts your manuscript it's time for more editing and once it's finally published, it's time for book marketing.

Section Seven Contents:

Writing Books for Children: From Contract to Working with the Editor to Sales to a Writing Career
Create Visibility Before Getting Published
Book Marketing: Visibility and Platform Basics
10 Essential Steps to an Effective Website
3 Keywords Needed to Create an Effective Website

Writing Books for Children: From Contract to Working with the Editor to Sales to a Writing Career

YOU'VE CHOSEN TO write books for children and you've done it by the books: you did your homework and learned the craft of writing, you created a polished manuscript, and you submitted it to publishers.

And, knowing it's not necessarily the best writer who gets published, but the one who perseveres, you were steadfast and didn't let initial rejections deter you.

Now, it's finally happened - all your hard work paid off. A publisher accepted your book and you're on your way.

But, this is far from the end of your writing journey ... this is just the beginning.

After your book is accepted for publication, there are three steps you will go through on your writing journey ... if you intend to make writing books for children a career:

1. Writing Books for Children: The Book Contract

You may want to sign that publishing contract as soon as you can, but be sure to read the contract carefully, if you don't understand something, ask for an explanation.

Once you're sure you understand everything in the contract and agree with it, sign away.

After you sign a contract, you'll be 'put in queue' and at some point begin editing with the publisher's editor. This will most likely involve more revisions.

From start to actual release, the publishing process can take 18 to 24 months.

2. Working with the publishing house editor

Once you're accepted by a publishing house, you will be assigned an editor. And don't be alarmed, but that manuscript you meticulously slaved over, and even paid an editor to go over, will end up with revisions. This is just the nature of the beast--each publishing house has their own way of doing things. They will want you're manuscript to fit their standards.

Note: the purpose of those long hours of writing work and hiring an editor is to give your manuscript the best shot of making it past the editor's trash can, and actually getting accepted.

Now on to 4 tips that will help make your editor/author experience a pleasant one:

Always be professional.

Don't get insulted when the editor requests revisions. They are not trying to hurt your feelings; they are hired by the publishing house to get your manuscript in the best possible sell-able state. They want your book to sell as much as you do.

Keep the lines of communication open. If you have a question, ask. If you disagree with an edit, respectfully discuss it. Editors are not infallible; sometimes your gut feeling is right.

Take note of deadlines and be on time--this is your career, and in some cases your livelihood.

3. Writing Books for Children: Book Promotion

When you start submitting your manuscript to publishers and agents, it's time to think of your author platform. You'll want to help promote your books to help with sales. This means creating visibility for you and your book.

You need to become a 'blip' on the internet radar through book marketing strategies.

Book promotion generates book sales.

The bare-bottom basics **of book promotion are:**

- Create a quality book
- Create an author website
- Have an opt-in box to build your subscriber list (mailing list)
- Offer a valuable gift (freebie) to entice visitors to your blog to sign-up to your mailing list
- Have a clear call to action

The main idea of promotion is to create and build visibility, traffic to your website, and a relationship with your readers.

After your book's release, you will want to take part in virtual book tours, create a press release, do blogtalk radio guest spots, school visits, and all the other standard book promotion strategies. You can take this on yourself, or you can hire a book promotion service or publicist.

If you do go with a promotion service or publicist, be sure to ask around for recommendations. You want to use a service or individual who knows what she's doing and who gives you value for your money.

4. Writing Books for Children: A Writing Career

Now, you've got your book and you're promoting it like crazy (this is an on-going process). The next step is to repeat the process, over and over and over.

You don't want to be a one-hit wonder, so hopefully you've been writing other stories while waiting to get a contract and then waiting for your book to be available for sale. If not, get started now. On average, an author writes a book every one to two years.

Along with keeping your *writing books for children* momentum up, having published books opens other writing opportunities, such as speaking engagements, conducting workshops, teleseminars, webinars, school visits, and coaching.

There are a number of marketers who say your 'book' is your business card or calling card. It conveys what you're capable of and establishes you as an expert in your field or niche. Take advantage of these additional avenues of visibility and income.

Create Visibility Before Getting Published

WE'RE GOING TO backtrack a bit and talk about what you should do before you get a contract.

What do you do while you're submitting your manuscript and waiting patiently? Okay, maybe not patiently, but waiting nonetheless.

This goes for self-publishing authors also. As you're writing your book or in the process of putting it all together, there's a lot you can be doing.

You need to start creating visibility. I don't mean standing on the street corner singing at the top of your lungs, I mean creating an online presence that depicts who and what you are. In other words, you need to create your author platform.

For those who aren't sure what a platform is, it is a means to let readers know about you and your books or what your area of expertise is.

Yes, I know, you might be shaking your head and thinking that you don't have an area of expertise, but this is how you create it.

As founder and editor-in-chief of Writers on the Move, I meet a number of writers who are reluctant to begin promoting themselves because they haven't landed a publisher yet. Or, they're still learning the craft. This mentality won't cut it today. You need to begin visibility right away.

First step in your platform journey is to create a website and blog (at the very least, an author website).

If you do have a blog, you'll want to write about the genre you're writing in. You can even blog about your manuscript's writing progress.

You might be wondering what the difference is between a website and a blog.

Well, a website can have a blog in it. But a blog, while kind of a website, doesn't have the functionality of a website.

The reason you might consider having a website with a blog is because a website allows you to have multiple webpages: About page, Book/s page/s, Media page, and so on.

These pages are considered static pages. Once they're created, they don't usually get changed. But they offer a visitor a lot of information about you and your book/s.

The blog on the other hand provides updated content in the form of blog posts on a regular basis and in chronological order. It doesn't have static pages.

This regular updating keeps your website active – this is good for search engines and people who visit.

The next step in your journey is to create your platform and online visibility. Learn your craft and as you're learning, write about what you learn. In other words, if your book is about cooking, blog about cooking – you will be creating your area of expertise.

The publishing and marketing industry has changed. In today's writing market publishing houses, big and small, expect you to:

1. Have and online presence (website)
2. Have a platform (what you and your books are about)
3. Have a social following
4. Have the potential to increase that following
5. Have a marketing strategy
6. Be able to sell your book

Book Marketing: Visibility and Platform Basics

Now we'll go into a bit more detail in regard to creating visibility and your platform.

Selling books today is a joint effort between the publishing house and the author.

And, if you're venturing into the self-publishing arena, promoting yourself is even more important. Don't procrastinate. You need to start creating your online presence and platform today.

Every author has thought it, said it, and heard it: promotion is the roll-up-your-sleeves, and dig-in part of writing, even more so than editing. It's the much more difficult and time consuming aspect of writing that every author needs to become involved with . . . if he wants to sell his books.

To actually sell a book, you need to have a quality product. This is the bare-bottom, first rung of book promotion . . . the foundation. And, a quality book includes cover and design.

Since this hasn't been discussed in the early sections, I'll touch on it now. It's an important topic for self-publishers.

The first thing is to create an effective title. It's a good idea to have a subtitle also. The title is the first thing a potential buyer will look at.

The second element that the reader will look at is the book cover and design.

The 'title and cover' is the first impression a reader will usually have of your book. And, it's essential to get this right. This is the time to invest in your book. Hire a professional to create a book cover for you. I used 100 Covers for the design of the front and back cover of this book. They're accommodating, very reasonably priced, and create great covers (at least in my opinion).

Don't skimp on time, effort, or money when coming up with your book's cover and design.

Next is the back cover. You will need back cover copy – this is a brief description of the story, but it needs to be written to motivate the reader to buy the book.

The copy should be no more than 200 words and needs to peak a reader's interest. You DON'T however want to divulge the ending / resolution to the story.

You might include a portion of an interior illustration (if you have a picture book) on the back cover. Or, research newly traditional published books in your genre and see how their back covers are designed.

Then there is the interior design. This is how the book looks and reads inside. You might consider hiring a self-publishing company to help you. Getting the formatting just right can be a pain.

All these pieces fit together to create a quality book.

NOW ON TO THE VISIBILITY AND PLATFORM BASICS

As mentioned, **the very first step in book promotion** is to create a quality product. Hopefully, you noticed I said create a *quality product*, not just a good story.

What this means is that all aspects of your book need to be top notch.

Creating the book might be considered Research and Development under the Marketing umbrella, and the foundation of a marketing strategy.

The second step or rung on the marketing ladder is the actual book promotion: creating a platform and brand for you and your book. This is accomplished through visibility.

What a platform is was already discussed, but this will give a little more detail.

1. Creating a Website/Blog

A. Your Domain Name

Choose your domain name carefully and think ahead. Marketing experts always advise using your name for your domain name. You can always create sites that are specific to each of your books or a particular niche, but your *name* should be your main or central site.

An example of a domain name: karencioffiwritingforchildren

The URL to that website (the address) is: http://karencioffiwritingforchildren.com

B. Choose a Website or Blog

There's no way around this one – you must create a web presence. The first tool in your visibility toolbox is a website, and it should be created while you're writing your book, well before it's published.

You can choose a website. You can get either type for free from sites such as Wordpress.com or Blogger.com.

If you find the thought of having to create a website daunting, go for Blogger. com; it'is very user friendly and good for beginners. And with its updates, it has features much like a website.

C. Simple is a Better Strategy

Marketing expert Mike Volpe of Hubspot.com points out that it's more important to spend time, and money if necessary, on content rather than a flashy website design. Simple works.

In fact, simpler usually leads to more sales.

Volpe also stresses that you should have control over your site. This means you should be able to manage it. You don't want to run to a web designer for every little change you want to make to your site, or to do something as simple as adding content.

To reinforce this *simple is better* strategy, Google says that milliseconds count in regard to your page load time. If your page is slow to load, you'll get a poorer score with Google and it could cause visitors to quickly bounce off your site.

Tip: Should you decide you do need help to create a site, don't hire an expensive web designer. Look for someone who wants to establish themselves as a website creator, or someone who does it in their spare time. You'll pay much less. And, try to make arrangements that will include the designer shows you how to manage your own site. This will make updates, changes, and posting much easier.

They'll be more on creating a website below.

2. Social Networking

This aspect of promotion should also be initiated prior to your book's publication. If you don't have social media accounts, start now.

A. Join the Biggies

It's important to become active on sites such as Twitter, Facebook, LinkedIn, Author's Den, and JacketFlap.

Twitter and Facebook are two of the biggest and powerful social networks.

You'll need to share blog posts to these sites regularly to draw attention and build on your visibility. You can also 'share' posts of other users that you find of interest or value. Those who follow you will appreciate the effort.

You should use social share buttons to make your blog posts shareable on your website. These 'share buttons' are usually located at the top or the bottom of the post. Be sure to make sharing your posts as easy as possible for visitors.

B. Join Pertinent Writing Forums and Groups

You should also join forums and groups related to the genre you're writing in. If you write science fiction join groups that provide discussions and tips in that genre. If you write for children join groups that are focused on that genre. You get the idea.

Tip: Be active on the sites. Offer information and share information you find valuable.

C. Join Groups Outside of the Writing Realm: Promotion and Your Target Market

It'd be a good idea to join groups that discuss promotion / marketing. You can also subscribe to sites that offer promotional information and tips. By doing this, new content added to the sites will be sent directly to your inbox.

Another strategy is to join forums that are interested in your book's topic (your target market). If you write science fiction, join sci-fi buff sites. If you write non-fiction cook books, join sites related to cooking. Try to be where the members/readers will find your book of interest and/or valuable.

3. Content Rules

Add Content to Your Blog

Make your presence known by offering information in the form of content on your blog. Content is what will make you noticeable.

But, just posting the content to your site will not create the traffic (visitors) you need. Each time you publish content (create a blog post) on your site, you need to let your social networks know about it.

Once your post is up, again post it to your social networks. When sharing your blog post, be sure to include a clickable URL link that goes directly back to the article on your website. This is a part of inbound marketing – it leads visitors back to your site through an information funnel.

Create Effective Blog Post Titles

Create titles that readers will want to click on.

Examples:

> Promote Your Book in 5 Easy Steps.
> Book Marketing in 5 Easy Steps
> Write a Book in 30 Days

These titles work well because the keywords are front and center (at the beginning).

Tip: Using content to draw visitors back to your site is inbound or organic marketing. It's free and it works by creating an information funnel leading back to your site. In order for inbound marketing to work effectively, you need to provide valuable content on a regular basis.

For the basics on SEO, I have a series at Writers on the Move that begins with:

SEO for Authors Series: The Basics
http://www.writersonthemove.com/2017/12/seo-for-authors-series-basics.html

8 Essential Steps to an Effective Website

MARKETING CAN BE a difficult journey. There's tons of competition. And, if you don't have a website, you won't be able to get in the marketing game.

No matter what product or service you're offering, having a website is an absolutely must.

While it's not that difficult to create a website or blogsite using services, such as WordPress (http://wordpress.com) or Blogger (http://blogger.com), there are essential steps you will need to take in order to create an EFFECTIVE site.

Here is a list of 8 of the most essential and bare-bottom basics that are needed for an effective website:

1. The Name of Your Site

We went over the domain name – this is about the title of your site.

You can use your domain name as the title, but you can also use something different.

My domain is karencioffiwritingforchildren, but the title of my site is:

Writing for Children with Karen Cioffi

And, I used a different name on the header-banner I created for my site:

Karen Cioffi, Children's Ghostwriter

A number of authors use their name and elaborate in the subheading.

2. The Subheading

When including a site subheading, think of your platform. In your subheading add keywords you want associated with your site. These are words that should quickly inform the search engines and visitors what your site is about.

An example is my children's writing site. The subheading has ghostwriting and rewriting in it. This is what the site is about.

3. The Opt-in Box

An opt-in box is text and an image that is used to get a visitor to your site to take action.

It could be to take action to subscribe to your mailing list or to buy your book.

Your first concern should be to get people to join your mailing list.

This opt-in is the primary tool to creating a mailing list. A useful way to entice visitors to sign up for your emails or newsletter is to offer a free gift. Usually an e-book or video related to your site's focus is a practical gift.

You could give a excerpt or a chapter of your book as a gift.

The opt-in box should be placed in the top portion of your sidebar, and must be immediately visible upon landing on the page – this means it needs to be above the fold line.

Above the fold line is what's visible when landing on your site without having to scroll down.

You can also include the email opt-in box at the bottom of each of your blog posts.

4. The 'About Me' or 'About Us' Page

Let the visitors know *who you are* with an About Page. This is especially important on sites that do not use the site owner's name as the title.

There are so many sites where a visitor needs to search to see who the site belongs to – it can be a bit frustrating, as well as a waste of the visitor's time. There are even some sites that don't offer this information, or it's possible the owners have it so well hid visitors can't find it.

Along with the names of the site contributors, you should let the visitors know what the site is about, what they can expect from the site, what information will provide.

The About Me Page should include a bio along with any pertinent schooling and/or training. Most visitors want to know who is posting the content and what qualifies them to offer that particular information.

Providing this information allows the reader to develop a relationship with you.

5. The Media Page

Create a Media Page. This page will tell visitors what you've written and other qualifications that make you an expert in your field.

You should also include your books, reviews of your work, brief descriptions and possibly excerpts, links to the sales pages, testimonials and awards, links to interviews others have written on you, events/workshops you've presented, your appearances, and links to all your other sites.

6. The Contact Page

Your contact information needs to be available. This means having a Contact Page that offers a contact form, or your email address. A visitor may have a question, comment, or request for your services. You want that visitor to be able to reach you.

On my site, I have my name, email address, and even my phone number on multiple pages and on my sidebar. This way it's super-easy to find.

7. Keep Your Site Focused

Keep the content you post to your site pertinent to your site's niche. Think of your site as a target -- you want to keep as close to the center of that target as possible.

So, if you're writing for children, keep your posts geared toward children's writing. If your site is about cooking, keep the posts geared to cooking related content.

If you begin to dilute your main focus, you will begin to lose credibility as an expert in a particular area. You don't want to be known as 'jack of all trades, master of none.'

8. Provide Valuable Content

Adding value CONTENT (blog posts) to your site is the number one marketing factor that will create relationships and make you an authority in your niche. Make your content informative and helpful and engaging to those reading it and they will return for more.

Also, be sure to post great content on a regular basis and promote each post through your social networks.

Why You Need an Email List

WITH ATTENTION SPANS dwindling and competition increasing, the main goal of your website is to get email addresses that convert into sales.

During an initial visit, your visitor may not have the time to spend browsing your site for information to entice him to make the decision to purchase your book or product.

And, marketing studies have shown that it takes around 7 touch points before a visitor will purchase a product. This means a first-time visitor to your website most likely won't buy your book. S/he needs at least another 6 or more connections to be motivated enough to buy.

This is where your mailing list comes in. You will be able to stay in touch with that visitor through a weekly or monthly newsletter. This builds a relationship that can turn into sales.

And, if you have a **FREE GIFT** offer for signing up, you've made the sign up decision even easier.

While it's important to offer that Free gift, which is considered an 'ethical bribe,' if it's of no value to the visitor, he probably won't bother signing up. So, how do you decide if your gift is valuable enough to grab that email address?

The answer to this question is easy: you know who your target buyers are. Think about it . . . what do they want? What would you want? If your site and product is about writing, guess what...your visitors would probably appreciate an ebook on that topic.

They may appreciate a how to write guide. Or, if you're into marketing...offer an ebook of marketing tips and guidance.

If your site is about cooking, offer recipes, or an instructional cooking ebook.

You could also offer a simple ebook on the topic of your book. For example, my middle-grade fantasy is set in ancient China. I could offer an ebook on the time period.

Or you can give away an excerpt of the book or even a chapter.

The idea is to make a connection.

So, that's pretty easy, right?

But, a word of caution here: make sure your new subscriber is able to get his free gift.

There are a couple of sites I've signed up to because I wanted the free offers. When I received the link to the offer, either the link didn't work, or I couldn't download the gift. Either way, I unsubscribe to the sites. I have on occasion sent an email to the site owner and ended up receiving the gift, but most often I don't bother. And, I'm sure others don't have the time to do this also.

Just a quick note here: you need an opt-in box in order to acquire those email addresses. Services such as iContact, GetResponse, and ConstantContact offer this service.

I use GetResponse – they're easy to use, reliable, and have great customer service. I'm an affiliate for them, so if you're looking to create a mailing list or you're thinking of changing your service, please use my link: http://www.getresponse.com/index/AWD1790

Two words that are essential to every website that is selling a book or other product are **BUY NOW**, or some other call-to-action. The call-to-action words or button needs to be visible and near the top of your home page. It should also be throughout your site on the sidebar.

Studies have shown over and over that only 1% of first time visitors will buy a product. It's usually after developing a relationship through your newsletter that your potential customer will click on the BUY NOW button!

You can actually sell your books right from your own site through services like PayPal. This should be of special interest to those of you who are venturing onto the self-publishing road.

This is the bare-bottom basics of book marketing. And, to fully understand how important it is in today's publishing arena take a look at this scenario:

If a publisher or agent is looking at two manuscripts of equal quality, one from someone with no platform or marketing skills and one from an author with a solid platform, who is social networking savvy, and has effective marketing skills, guess which author will get the contract?

Publishers and agents are in the book business to sell books – they want their authors to be able to help with that process. So, become a savvy book marketer.

The next section of this book is the last one and is all about additional resources to help you on your writing and book marketing journey.

Section
Eight

Lots of Writing and Marketing Bonus Resources

SINCE LEARNING TO *write and market your books is an ongoing process I've in-cluded A LOT of additional resources to help give you every advantage to creating a successful writing career. What's amazing about the internet is if you visit one site, you can find links to other amazing and informative sites, articles, books, etc.*

Please note, sites online can disappear overnight, so I don't guarantee the links will work.

Section Eight Contents
    Helpful Online Sites
    Writing Article Links
    Writing Resources and Online Tools
    Books and eBooks
    Writing and Marketing Programs, eCourses, and Services
    The End and a Bonus Article: Picture Book or Children's Magazine Article?
    Quotes

Helpful Online Sites

NOTE: In the revision to this book, since it will be available in paperback in addition to digital format, I created a Resources for Writers page on my website. It's under the DIY option in the menu.

The link is: http://karencioffiwritingforchildren.com/diy/resources-for-writers/

Or, just go to my website and click on the DIY button in the menu. A drop down menu will appear and it's there you'll find Resources for Writers.

The Resources page includes:

Writing Blogs
Literary Agent Blogs
Publishing and Book Marketing Blogs
Self-Publishing Services
Writing Resources and Online Tools
Writing and Marketing Groups, Programs, and Services

Writing Article Links

THE PROS AND Cons of Publishing with a Small Publisher
http://www.writersdigest.com/editor-blogs/guide-to-literary-agents/pros-cons-publishing-small-press

How to Find Writing Workshops
http://www.writersonthemove.com/2012/03/how-to-find-writing-workshops-seminars.html

What I Learned from the Movie "Young Adult"
http://www.writersonthemove.com/2012/03/what-i-learned-from-movie-young-adult.html

Critique Guidelines for Happy Writers by Carolyn Howard-Johnson
http://www.writersonthemove.com/2012/03/carolyns-critique-guidelines-for-happy.html

Grammar Tips with Anne Duguid
http://www.writersonthemove.com/2012/02/writing-daily-dozen.html

Difference Between Style and Voice
http://www.writersonthemove.com/2012/02/difference-between-style-and-voice-by.html

When You Are a Beginning Writer, The Keyword is Focus
http://pubrants.blogspot.com/2012/01/when-you-are-beginning-writer-keyword.html

Don't Even Think About Using First-Person Unless . . .
http://wordplay-kmweiland.blogspot.com/2012/02/dont-even-think-about-using-first.html

100 Words for Facial Expressions
http://www.dailywritingtips.com/100-words-for-facial-expressions/

Want to Self-Publish a Rhyming Children's Book? Read This First
http://karencioffiwritingforchildren.com/2016/05/29/want-to-self-publish-a-rhyming-childrens-book-read-this-first/

4 Realities New Writers Need to Face
http://karencioffiwritingforchildren.com/2016/05/15/4-realities-new-writers-need-to-face/

Writing a Book – To Traditionally Publish or To Self-Publish
http://karencioffiwritingforchildren.com/2016/07/24/writing-a-book-to-publish-traditionally-or-self-publish/

Books and eBooks

ON WRITING

Bird by Bird
Author: Anne Lamott
Here's a quote from the New York Times Book Review: "Superb writing advice...hilarious, helpful and provocative."

Stephen King – On Writing: A Memoir of the Craft
Author: Stephen King
This book offers insight and instruction on the craft of writing.

Children's Writers Word Book
Author: Alijandra Mogilner and Tayopa Mogilner
This book lists words in groups by grades; provides a thesaurus of those words; provides detailed guidelines for sentence length, word usage, and themes at each reading level; and more. It's a very hand book to have if you're writing for children.

The New Rhyming Dictionary
Author: Sue Young
Includes phrases, buzz words, and American slang

Metaphors Dictionary
Author: Elyse Sommer with Dorrie Weiss
It provides 6,500 comparative phrases, including 800 Shakespearean metaphors.

Descriptionary – A Thematic Dictionary
Author: Marc McCutcheon
This book can help you when you know what it is, but not what it's called.

The Analogy Book of Related Words – Your Secret Shortcut to Power Writing
Author: Selma Glasser
This book is a valuable aid for all who seek to create powerful prose. It has 78 lists of related words; plus examples on how to use them.

The Synonym Finder
Author: J. I. Rodale

As One Mad With Wine and Other Similes
Author: Elyse Sommer and Mike Sommers
This book provides more than 8,000 similes coined by nearly 2,000 sources ranging from Arabian Nights to the Bible to popular television shows and computer bulletin boards.

Breathing Life Into Your Characters
Author: Rachel Ballon, Ph. D.
How to give your characters emotional and psychological depth

Crafting Scenes
Author: Raymond Obstfeld

Yes! You Can Learn How to Write Children's Books, Get Them :Published, and Build a Successful Writing Career
Author: Nancy I. Sanders
Writing time and focus management strategies, secrets to landing a contract, and much more from award-winning and multi-published (80+) author.

ON EDITING

The Frugal Editor
Author: Carolyn Howard-Johnson
This book takes you through the writing process from start to finish. It's provides easy-to-understand and valuable advice, tips, information, and resources.

The Little, Brown Essential Handbook, 6th Ed.
Author: Jane E. Aaron

The Great Grammar Book: Mastering Grammar Usage and the Essentials of Composition by Marsha Sramek
The book provides information about grammar. It includes explanations, great examples, and reviews. It focuses on only those grammatical terms which are necessary to avoid mistakes or to improve writing skills.

The Elements of Style by William Strunk, Jr.

The Chicago Manual of Style

MBL Handbook for Writers by Joseph Gibaldi

ON MARKETING

The Frugal Book Promoter – How to Do What Your Publisher Won't
By Carolyn Howard-Johnson
This book is jammed packed with advice, tips, and information about promotion.

Red Hot Internet Publicity – An Insider's Guide to Marketing Your Book on the Internet
By Penny C. Sansevieri
This book provides an in depth look at internet marketing.

Please note that on marketing books, you need the most current editions as marketing strategies change often and can change quickly.

If after reading this book, you found it helpful, I would appreciate it if you give this book an Amazon review. Reviews help sell books – your review would be appreciated.

~~~~~

Still feel you need help with your story? Let's discuss your project. You can email me at kcioffiventrice@gmail.com.

The End

THERE IS A lot of information in this book, especially with the online resources, and hopefully it will guide you on your children's writing path.

But, this is just the beginning. Keep writing as much as you can, whenever you can. Follow the instructions in this book and you should steadily hone your writing craft.

While this book deals specifically with children's fiction writing for books, you can also write children's fiction articles. In fact, you can 'dip your toe' in the publishing waters with submissions to children's magazines, if you feel writing a full book is a bit daunting.

But, remember, just as with publishing houses, you need to read each magazine's guidelines carefully.

Here's a brief article on the differences between a book and an article:

PICTURE BOOK OR CHILDREN'S MAGAZINE ARTICLE?

Since the word counts may be the same for a picture book and magazine article, it's important to determine what the actual differences are between a picture book and a children's magazine article.

When writing for young children the format and storyline are not usually interchangeable—meaning they are usually geared toward a picture book or article.

Some of the Characteristics of a Picture Book:

A picture book is written to allow for illustrations.

It has a 50/50 ratio of content and illustrations.

The illustrations actually help tell the story.

The storyline is one that includes the 3 levels: surface, underlying meaning, and take away value.

New information may be found with additional readings.

A picture book is created to be read over and over and over. And, it is often handed down to younger siblings.

Some of the Characteristics of a Children's Magazine Article:

A children's article is written complete. Illustrations are not used to add to the story.

It may have one or two illustrations.

It doesn't have to include the 3 levels of picture books.

It's read once or twice and then usually discarded.

Allowing for Illustrations in a Picture Book

When writing a picture book (PB), the author needs to think about the illustrations. Since PBs are usually 32 pages, you need to allow for a minimum of 13 illustrations. This will affect the way you write your sentences. You don't have to express everything. If Tommy hits the ball and gets a home run, you don't have to say the ball flew over the fence.

Or, if Luke grabs his bat and ball, but forgets his cleats, you don't have to actually say he forgot his cleats. The illustrator will reflect this with a wonderful picture that shows more than you thought possible.

To help you envision how your PB will look and how the content and illustrations will work, you should **create a Dummy Book**. This will help you see where the breaks should be and if you need to rewrite to make it all work.

*****

I hope this book provides you with a strong foundation for all your writing endeavors. I've added some inspiring quotes below.

One final tip: If you need help creating and managing your author platform, visit: **Build Your Author/Writer Platform**

http://wow-womenonwriting.com/classroom/KarenCioffi_WebsiteTrafficInboundMarketing.php

(It's a 4-week, in-depth, interactive eclass through WOW! Women on Writing)

Karen Cioffi

Quotes

BEFORE I GET into the quotes, I'd like to emphasis how important book reviews are – they're an essential part of book marketing.

If you've found this book helpful, I would appreciate it if you would leave a review on Amazon. If you're familiar with Goodreads, it'd be great if you'd publish your review there also.

As I didn't mention it before, after your book is published, whether traditionally or self-published, ask for book reviews.

Ask peers, friends, family, and anyone else you can think of. Don't be shy about this. Book reviews help sell books.

Okay, on to the writing and life quotes.

ON WRITING

"Imagination is more important than knowledge. Knowledge is limited. Imagination encircles the world." ~ *Albert Einstein*

"A writer who never gives up is called Published." ~ *J.A. Konrath*

"Good luck is another name for tenacity of purpose." ~ *Ralph Waldo Emerson*

"Talent is cheaper than table salt. What separates the talented individual from the successful one is a lot of hard work." ~ *Stephen King*

"Don't tell me the moon is shining; show me the glint of light on broken glass." ~ *Anton Chekhov*

"The difference between the right word and the almost right word is the difference between lightning and a lightning bug." ~ *Mark Twain*

"Easy reading is damn hard writing." ~ *Nathaniel Hawthorne*

"I didn't have time to write a short letter, so I wrote a long one instead." ~ *Mark Twain*

"Anyone can become a writer. The trick is staying a writer." ~ *Harlan Ellison*

"It's none of their business that you have to learn how to write. Let them think you were born that way." ~ *Ernest Hemingway*

"The more you read, the more you will write. The better the stuff you read, the better the stuff you will write." ~ *Annie Dillard*

"Don't use words too big for the subject. Don't say 'infinitely' when you mean 'very'; otherwise you'll have no word left when you want to talk about something really infinite." ~ *C. S. Lewis*

ON LIFE AND SUCCESS

"Dost thou love life? Then do not squander time, for that's the stuff life is made of." ~ *Benjamin Franklin*

"It's not what you've done that matters - it's what you haven't done."
~ *Mark Twain*

"The harder I work, the luckier I get" ~ *Samuel Goldwyn*

"If a man empties his purse into his head no one can take it away from him. An investment in knowledge always pays the best interest." ~ *Benjamin Franklin*

"Don't spend time beating on a wall, hoping to transform it into a door."
~ *Dr. Laura Schlessinger*

"Nothing is impossible, the word itself says I'M POSSIBLE." ~ *Audrey Hepburn*

"Even if you're on the right track, you'll get run over if you just sit there."
~ *Will Rogers*

"You have brains in your head. You have feet in your shoes. You can steer yourself in any direction you choose." ~ *Dr. Seuss*

"You don't win an Olympic gold medal with a few weeks of intensive training."
~ *Seth Godin, Author*

"If your ship doesn't come in, swim out to it." ~ *Jonathan Winters*

"Don't let your learning lead to knowledge; let your learning lead to action."
~ *Jim Rohn*

About the Author

KAREN CIOFFI IS an award-winning children's author, working children's ghostwriter with over 200 clients worldwide, a former lead editor with 4RV Publishing, a former online learning center fiction staff writer, and an author online platform instructor with WOW! Women on Writing.

Karen's memberships include:

Association of Ghostwriters
Professional Writers Alliance
National Association of Independent Writers and Editors
Freelancers Union
Society of Children's Book Writers and Illustrators (SCBWI)
JacketFlap and Author's Den

You can connect with Karen at:

https://karencioffiwritingforchildren.com
https:writersonthemove.com
LinkedIn: http://www.linkedin.com/in/karencioffiventrice
Facebook: https://www.facebook.com/writingforchildrenwithkarencioffi/
Twitter: https://twitter.com/KarenCV

CPSIA information can be obtained
at www.ICGtesting.com
Printed in the USA
BVHW041011040222
627985BV00015B/468